IN DEEP WATER

'You'll be scared of water for the rest of your life,' Nicola told Jan, 'if you don't do some-thing about it . . .'

A boating accident has left Jan terrified of water, reluctant to face up to her fear. But when Nicola takes up synchro-swimming Jan allows herself to be talked round—provided her friend will be around to encourage and help.

When Nicola finds a new interest— good-looking Kerry—Jan is devastated. There's the swimming gala coming up, so she has to stay in the synchro team, but she knows she can't cope at the pool on her own. Until Clemmie comes to the rescue.

VERONICA HELEY lives in London and is the author of thirty books for children and adults. In addition, she writes book reviews and short stories, runs a holiday club for children and until recently also led a youth club.

Louise

In Deep Water

Veronica Heley

Veronica Heley (signature)

A LION PAPERBACK

Oxford · Batavia · Sydney

Copyright © 1992 Veronica Heley

The right of Veronica Heley to be identified as the
author of this work has been asserted by her in accordance
with the Copyright, Designs and Patents Act 1988.

Published by
Lion Publishing plc
Sandy Lane West, Oxford, England
ISBN 0 7459 2399 2
Albatross Books Pty Ltd
PO Box 320, Sutherland, NSW 2232, Australia
ISBN 0 7324 0584 X

First edition 1992

Author's note:
There is no such charity as the International Children's Fund.
Several charities do work such as that described in this story,
some working in the UK and some concentrating on work
abroad.
Thanks are due to the Amateur Swimming Association for their
kind help, to the synchro team at St Paul's School, London, and
to the synchro team at Plymouth Leander Club, Plymouth.

A catalogue record of this book is available
from the British Library

Printed and bound in Great Britain
by Cox & Wyman Ltd, Reading

Contents

1
Nightmares

The weeds had got me. They wound themselves tightly round my foot, so tightly that pain shot up my leg. I couldn't fight any longer. I was going to die.

My head filled with a red balloon which turned to black as I went down . . .

. . . and woke up choking.

Shivering in the night cold.

I huddled under the bedclothes, trying to breathe normally. I had thrashed the duvet askew and had cramp in my left foot.

I told myself I was breathing in air and not water. It had been three years and eleven months since the accident. If I still got scared when I looked at water, well, I was doing something about it, wasn't I? Soon the nightmares would stop and everything would be all right again.

I had left the curtains open a crack and the street light shone across my bed and as far as the door. I wriggled my foot around, but it was no good. I had to get out of bed and stamp around.

I tried not to make a noise. The central heating had switched itself off, and the air was sharp. My little clock showed it was two in the morning. Time for me to have the nightmare again several times before morning, if I didn't do something about it.

I could creep downstairs to get myself some milk and chocolate biscuits. Problem: the parents slept with their door open. Mum slept lightly, and it wasn't likely I'd get down the stairs without waking her. I didn't want her coming in and talking about it, all anxious and making silly suggestions. It was bad enough having the nightmare without people wanting to talk about it.

So, scrub going downstairs. I remembered I had a Kit-Kat in my school bag, left over from lunch. As the cramp eased, I retrieved the chocolate and ate it, slowly, making every crumb last and licking my fingers afterwards. I'd read somewhere that carbohydrates act as painkillers. That's why they give you lots of sugar in your tea if you've had a shock.

Well, I hadn't had a shock. It had been a blip, not a shock. A blip on the screen of my life. I was used to blips. I could cope.

I thought about turning on the light and reading for a bit, but I hadn't a decent book to read, only something from school about the First World War, and you couldn't read that for comfort. What I wanted was carbohydrate-type reading. Something sweet and sustaining. Something about a girl overcoming her problems and ending up the most popular girl in the school. As if.

No, well, I knew that wasn't likely to happen to me, but I *was* going to beat my nightmare if it killed me.

Tomorrow ... no, it was today, wasn't it? ... Nicola had promised me faithfully that she'd turn up for early morning practice at the swimming pool. She hadn't been able to make the last couple of times, so all I'd been able to do was pootle up and down practising sculling in half a dozen different ways. Any way so long as I didn't have to put my head under water. I *never* put my head under water unless Nicola was there. Or our coach, Debbie. She didn't know I was afraid of water, but I could trust her to rescue me if I got into difficulties.

Going under water, weeds, ugh. Sometimes I only had to look at the surface of the pool, and it would turn into a fast flowing river, streaked with weeds . . .

I turned my mind from it. I would *not* let the fear beat me. But at times like this, in the darkest part of the night, I wondered if it had been altogether wise to sign up for synchro-swimming. Left to myself, it would never have occurred to me to do it. My own idea had been to keep as far away from water as possible.

But Nicola had fallen in love with synchro-swimming, and nothing would satisfy her but that we both sign up for it.

'I'm just dying to try it,' she said. 'It's magic, like dancing in the water. We've both done ballet and swimming, but synchro's just so much more exciting!'

At first I'd said No, but she'd talked me round. She'd said I'd be scared of water for the rest of my life if I didn't do something about it. Besides which, she was my best friend, and we always did everything together, didn't we?

'Look,' she said. 'What can go wrong if I'm always there with you? I promise I'll help you with the underwater bits. And we can do extra practice together and get you used to it little by little. We can make it a sort of treat and reward ourselves. I know, they sell delicious hot chocolate at the pool. You've always got enough money for hot chocolate, haven't you? Yum, I do love it, and we never get it at home.'

'Yes, but what if doing synchro-swimming makes my nightmares worse?'

'I promise you it won't. Oh, come on! Sign on the dotted line.'

So I signed my name neatly, Janet Wakeman, and she signed a big squiggly Nicola C., not bothering to fill in her full name because everyone knew who Nicola Callender was.

We had started off all right last September, and I thought I had not been doing too badly on the whole, while Nicola had really enjoyed it. It had become a sort of ritual, Nicola and me working on the figures together and, just before we got out, my going under water while she counted how long I could manage to stay there. And then we would go for a hot chocolate drink afterwards.

But then for some reason she'd stopped coming to early morning practices and I'd begun to worry about going under water again. And the nightmares had come back.

Well, if Nicola couldn't make it for early morning practice today, I'd remind her when we got to our afternoon swimming lesson. Perhaps we could both stay on afterwards to work on underwater figures. Not for long, perhaps only ten minutes. I had enough money to buy her a chocolate egg as well as a chocolate drink afterwards.

I scrabbled under the duvet and closed my eyes. I whispered, It's going to be all right, I'm going to beat it, I am, I am, I am . . .

I changed into my swimming costume, located my earplugs and nose-clip, but couldn't find my goggles. The main rush of people had gone and the changing room was empty except for Nicola and myself.

Nicola was pottering around, pulling her long hair up and back. She's got a cloud of light brown hair which looks as if it's been permed, but hasn't. I wish my hair were like that. Although it's blonde, mine is dead straight and there's nothing you can do with it except tie it back out of the way.

I didn't like to remind Nicola she'd missed so many early morning sessions, because she got really angry if you criticised her for anything. I had to word it just right.

'Nicola, if you're not having to rush away after, do you think . . .?'

She didn't seem to have heard me. 'Does this way of doing my hair suit me best, or on one side?'

'One side is more interesting. Listen, I've got some money for a hot drink and some chocolate, if you can stay on a bit afterwards.'

'You don't think it makes me look scraggy like this?'

'No, it's nice. I've been practising sculling, but I don't like to do anything else unless you're there.'

'I can't always be with you. Can't you do it by yourself?'

'You know I can't. You promised me that . . .'

'I never *promised*.'

I gaped at her. 'But Nicola, you did!'

'No, I never. Promised what, anyway? You do go on so, Jan. You're getting to be a real pain.'

A nasty hard place was growing in my stomach.

She said, 'The trouble with you is, you never think

11

of anyone but yourself. I've got problems, too, you know.'

'You should have told me. What's wrong?'

A big sigh. 'There you are, you see. You haven't been listening to anything I've said. I told you. How many more times?'

I tried to remember what she'd been talking about recently. She wasn't particularly happy at home, because her Dad grumbled at everything and her young brother was a pain, but I couldn't remember her complaining about them much lately. On the other hand, she had gone on a bit about a party she wanted to go to.

'You mean the party?'

She sighed again. 'You actually remembered? I'm counting the hours, and you can't even remember why? Honest, Jan, you're the absolute end.'

'Was it because Kerry asked you?'

'Now you remember!'

'What's wrong, then? I thought you liked him.'

'I don't *like* him! I *love* him! Don't you ever listen to anything I say? I can't think why I bother to go around with you, I really can't.' She slammed her locker door and left.

It took me a while to get myself together. Nicola couldn't have meant it, of course. She'd be back in a minute. She never would apologize for anything. That wasn't her way. No, she'd burst in and say something funny, and then I'd laugh and everything would be all right again.

She couldn't have meant it.

Why, we'd been friends for ever! They'd even called us the 'heavenly twins' in Middle School because we'd been inseparable, and were both small, thin and fair. Nicola had grown faster than I had done and, while I was still on the small side, she was now much taller and bigger in every way.

She didn't come back.

'Hurry up! Debbie's waiting!' Someone yelled into the changing room. You didn't keep our coach waiting, not if you knew what was good for you. I slammed my locker door and ran off to the pool.

The pool is nice. Modern. Actually there are four pools: there's a shallow basin for toddlers, and then two big swimming pools which can be made into one so that you can do proper lengths. Right at the end there's the diving pit which is where the synchro-swimming is done. It's smaller than the others, of course, but much deeper. There is a very wide surround to the diving pool, which they call 'the deck'.

All the other members of the synchro squad were already there, earplugs in, nose-clips on, pulling on their goggles. Debbie was dropping the special sound equipment into the water and plugging it into the portable cassette recorder.

I hovered on the edge. Sometimes I can be near water and hardly feel afraid at all, but after that row with Nicola just looking at the water made me feel quivery. I knew what to do about it, of course. Breathe in, count five, breath out, count five . . .

I tried to breathe in and hold it but couldn't. The loss of my goggles was the last straw. I couldn't go in without them. I hadn't been wearing goggles when the accident happened, so they acted as a sort of safety device, distancing me from everything that could hurt me. Like putting a pane of glass between me and a shark in an aquarium.

'Please,' I tried to attract Debbie's attention.

'What is it, Jan? Hurry up, everyone's waiting for you.'

'I can't find my goggles.'

'Well, you'll have to manage without them, just for once.' She turned to a girl who was doing cartwheels along the deck at the very edge of the pool. 'Clemmie, don't do that. It's stupid. Suppose you missed your footing and fell in. You could hurt yourself and anyone you happened to fall on.'

'OK, no sweat,' said Clemmie, doing her usual good-natured act. She was a lovely cocoa colour with dark hair and eyes. Today she was wearing a scarlet swimsuit which looked smashing on her. She was about as good at synchro-swimming as I was—which wasn't saying much—but she always looked as if she were enjoying herself.

'Hurry up, Jan! One quick run round the deck, and into the water,' said Debbie.

I hung back, shivering. Nicola was already in the water and talking to another girl. Was she deliberately not looking at me?

'Look!' said Clemmie, 'Here's some goggles on the floor. I think Nicola dropped them. You can borrow them, can't you?'

She jumped into the water with a horrible splash and got shouted at by everyone else.

They were *my* goggles. Nicola must have taken them by mistake for her own and dropped them when she realized they weren't hers. I ran round the deck to warm up and dropped neatly into the water.

We started off as usual by sculling, using only our hands to propel us along. We did one width forwards, and one width on our backs. Then we had to do sculling with a ballet leg—that's with one leg up out of the water, toes pointed—and so on. All that was getting easier for me, because I'd done so much practice.

I wanted to make it up with Nicola, but she still wouldn't look at me.

Clemmie did an oyster, which is sort of collapsing yourself in the middle and going down with fingers touching toes. Of course that wasn't what we were supposed to be doing at that moment, so she got shouted at by Debbie. No one could understand why Clemmie wanted to do synchro-swimming. She just wasn't a natural swimmer, and that's all there was to it. The other girls used to thin their lips and look patient when Clemmie was playing up, but I thought she was good fun.

Why was Nicola behaving like this? It was so unlike her.

We practised sculling in circles for a while but I kept getting out of place and so did Clemmie. At last Debbie shouted at us two to go and do some sculling games while the others practised figures.

Nicola still wasn't looking at me.

I felt sore at being told off, but glad that I didn't have to put my head under water. Practising with Clemmie was fun because she just couldn't seem to help laughing, no matter what we did. And when she concentrated, we actually got some of it right.

The others were doing dolphin somersaults, first by themselves and then in pairs. Nicola got out because she had cramp but pointedly turned her back on me. Then Anoushka—our star swimmer—got cramp as well, so we all took a breather.

Debbie said the new swimming costumes for the

squad had arrived and, if we had the money, we could pay her now. Most of us went back to the changing room to get our purses.

My purse was there but, to my horror, the twenty-pound note Mum had given me to pay for the costume had gone. There was my watch, and there were the couple of pound coins which I'd taken out of my money box for our chocolate treats. I knew the note had been there earlier, because I'd seen it when I'd put my watch in.

I couldn't believe it. 'Some of my money's gone!'

'It can't have. You've put it somewhere else.'

'No, I haven't.'

'What's the matter?' asked Debbie. I told her, and she looked grim. I thought she was going to say I'd made a mistake, too, but she didn't.

I had an inspiration. 'Nicola knew I'd got a twenty-pound note. I showed her.'

'Did you?' Nicola smiled at Debbie and shrugged. That hurt.

Clemmie said, or rather muttered, 'I saw Jan had a note in her purse. I saw when she put her watch in, when we were all changing.'

Nicola laughed, not nicely. 'Hard up this week, Clemmie?'

Clemmie looked furious, but Debbie held up her hand. 'OK, so Jan had some money and it's gone. There's been no one in this changing room tonight except us. Suppose we all look to see if we've got some money we shouldn't have.'

'That's stupid!' said Nicola. 'Why should *I* have her money?'

'Because a silly prank went wrong?' Debbie made it a suggestion, but the look she gave Nicola made me shiver.

'Nicola's my best friend,' I said. 'She wouldn't do a thing like that.'

'I haven't got her money!' shouted Nicola, bright red in the face.

I couldn't think why she was so upset. My own face was getting red. I said, 'It couldn't be Nicola, not possibly . . .'

'Nevertheless . . .' Debbie picked up Nicola's school bag.

I expected Nicola to open it and show she hadn't got the money, but she didn't. She looked as if she were going to cry. And then . . . then she dived into the bag, pulled out a twenty-pound note and threw it at me!

2
Betrayed!

'Take your stupid money!' said Nicola. 'I only borrowed it, anyway.'

I couldn't believe it! Nicola, my very best friend of all . . . Nicola had stolen my money?

Debbie picked up the note and said something sharp to Nicola.

Nicola's voice went high and clear, justifying herself. 'I only took it for a joke. She would have to make a fuss, wouldn't she, when it was only a joke!'

'I don't think Jan appreciated that it was only a joke,' said Debbie. 'And if it was a joke, then I think it was in very poor taste. How about an apology, Nicola?'

'For a *joke*? She took it the wrong way, that's all. And anyway, I don't know why you're going on about it. Jan's got so much money, she doesn't know what to do with it. She's always making a big deal about buying me chocolate. She deserves . . .'

'That's enough!' snapped Debbie. 'Apologize, or else!'

I heard myself say, 'Oh, no!'

'I'm sorry!' said Nicola, but she said it in such a way that I knew she would rather have sworn at me instead.

My whole life had been turned upside down in the space of a few minutes. I sat down on the bench in a hurry. Debbie said it was time for us to pack up for the evening, but that she wanted to see Nicola and me for a moment before we left.

The others were very quiet as they showered and got dressed. There wasn't any attempt at talking, just the odd mutter. Nicola made a big production of getting changed. She spoke to a couple of the other girls. They looked at her sideways and said Yes or No and that was all. One by one they began to slip away.

I realized I couldn't just sit there all night, so I got up and went over to the lockers. Everything seemed unreal. I stumbled into my clothes and pushed a comb through my hair.

'Are you all right?' asked Clemmie. She was holding out the money which had caused all the trouble. I took it from her and put it back in my purse. Everyone else had gone, even Nicola.

Clemmie repeated herself, 'Are you sure you're all right?'

I nodded. She hesitated but went away. I tried not to cry, but it was no use. The tears just poured out.

After a while Debbie came back in, dragging Nicola after her. I turned my head away and mopped myself up.

Nicola said, 'You see, she just has to cry, no matter what!'

'Now come on, I thought you two were best friends.'

'We used to go around together when we were kids. Now, well, she's just such a baby, and I've grown out of all that stuff. I've tried to tell her that I've got other friends now, but she just won't take the hint.'

I couldn't speak. It was all I could do not to start crying again. I kept my face turned away from her. I felt ashamed, and guilty. Was it true? Had she really grown out of our friendship? And hadn't I noticed when she'd tried to tell me?

To think I'd woken up that morning planning what we'd do, and thinking about buying her extra chocolate and walking home together just as we always did! She'd been my best friend for so long, and neither of us had ever bothered with anyone else! Suddenly the world was a very cold, unfriendly place.

Debbie said, 'Well, Nicola, I don't think much of the way you've behaved to Jan. The joke you played on her—if it was a joke and not just plain stealing—was in very poor taste. If Jan wanted to press charges, we could bring the police in . . .'

'Oh, no!' I said. I tried to look at Nicola, but her face was just a blur. Maybe that was just as well. I could imagine how she was looking at me, as if she hated me. She must have hated me, mustn't she, to have done such a thing?

'Then I suggest,' said Debbie, 'that you two go and have a hot drink together, and talk it over. Friends shouldn't fall out like this, should they? All right, Jan?'

'Yes,' I said, but I guessed that Nicola wasn't going to do it.

Debbie watched us walk out of the changing room and up the stairs to the viewing gallery where there is a small coffee bar. Nicola walked ahead of me and kept on going to the toilets at the far end. I got some chocolate and a hot drink and sat down, waiting for her to come back.

I'd finished my drink before I remembered that

there was another door out of the toilets, back on to the main staircase. I don't think I'd really expected her to join me, because I'd only bought one drink and one bar of chocolate.

I wondered if Debbie would come to check up on us, but she didn't. I began the long slog home. It was getting dark, but there were plenty of people around and the streets were well lit. Usually Nicola and I walked as far as the corner of my road together. It was weird being alone.

I got home and crept indoors. My younger brother Chas and two of his friends were watching TV in the living room. Chas is OK, I suppose, if you like loud-mouthed know-it-alls. He's popular at school, and on the whole he leaves me alone, so I suppose things could be worse. I was thankful they were making a lot of noise tonight, so that I could slip in unnoticed. I couldn't have told the parents what had happened without crying again.

When I went downstairs later, Mum was in the kitchen with Dad. He was opening a bottle of wine. They were arguing about what we should do for half term and didn't really look at me while I did my usual chores.

I hadn't thought I could eat, but I made myself do so or Mum would have had the thermometer out (or even her tomahawk if I let on what had happened between Nicola and me). I didn't know which would be worse; her fussing over me, or her going on the warpath to Nicola's.

I couldn't bear to think about what had happened, it hurt so much. But I couldn't stop thinking about it, either.

I kept going over and over it in my mind . . . Nicola

opening her school bag and throwing the money at me . . . Nicola saying that we weren't best friends and hadn't been for some time.

I went upstairs, got my books out and tried to work. But I couldn't.

I kept seeing her face. I just didn't understand how she could change like that.

Life really was awful.

I woke up and looked at the sunshine falling in a band across my duvet. Then I remembered, and it was like dropping into a deep dark pit.

Oh well, I said to myself. Just another blip on the screen of my life. Best get on with it. Mind you, any more blips and this machine will be marked 'Temporarily out of order'.

I got up when Mum yelled at me. I washed and dressed and ate breakfast just as if it was any ordinary day. I even managed to finish off my maths while Mum and Dad sorted out who was going to which committee meeting that night and what time supper would be.

Chas was groaning. Said he had tummy-ache. Mum got agitated, then she saw he was winking at me and shot him off with an earful. We went out of the house together, but he soon ran on ahead to meet his friends at the corner of the road. It wasn't far to school, and we usually walked.

Sometimes Nicola took the bus to school and I met her there, but occasionally her dad dropped her off at the corner of our road on his way in to work, and then we'd walk on together. Today I paused at the corner. I had hoped she'd got over her tantrum and would be waiting there, cracking jokes to show she was sorry.

Then we could have linked arms and gone on to school together as we always had done in the past.

There was no one waiting for me at the corner. I did up the top button of my school blouse. The wind was cold today.

Ours was a big school, fee-paying but with quite a lot of scholarships. Parents fought to get us in and sometimes went without things to keep us there. I'd moved up only this year into the High School—with Nicola. We'd been going around together since we were put on the same table in Middle School.

The Middle School was just down the road. I watched Chas race into the Middle School grounds to join up with his friends. He never seemed to have any problems. They said he might even get a scholarship to the High School.

It was one of those pure clear days in Spring when everything looks fresh, like a watercolour. The amber stone of the school buildings looked as if it had been freshly scrubbed, and all the windows gleamed. There was masses of green space around the buildings. A belt of shrubs hid the newer arts and science blocks, and the sports hall which we shared with the Middle School.

We didn't have our own swimming pool, but had a special arrangement to use the facilities at the Leisure Centre across the main road.

Our synchro-swimming coach, Debbie Wright, was actually on the staff of our school. She was in charge of our school's ordinary swimming lessons and, because she specialized in synchro, she'd formed the Synchro Squad as well. This met as a club after school on Wednesdays. The members of the Squad were drawn from several different schools locally, and we were allowed access to the diving pool for practice sessions early in the morning and after school at special rates.

I didn't want to think about the diving pool. That part of my life had ended the previous evening.

Someone pushed past me, and I realized I was going to be late if I didn't get a move on. I walked quickly through into the playground.

And there another problem came up and hit me. How could I go into school as if nothing had happened? I couldn't face sitting next to Nicola any more... not that I supposed she'd want to sit next to me.

I went into assembly and H.H.—that's His Highness, our Headteacher—got up and started talking about the importance of sport in our daily lives. Today of all days. According to him, playing games and eating sensible food gave you a healthy body, which was the foundation of a healthy life.

We call him H.H. because he always uses the royal 'we' instead of 'I'.

'*We* never cheat at games, do we?' and all that. I don't think I'd heard him say 'I', ever.

H.H. switched without pause from talking about sport to the equal importance of wearing proper uniform, having good manners and neat handwriting. I couldn't see Nicola. I wondered if she was right and I had been well, tactless, in giving her sweets and offering to stand treats all the time? The thing was that I knew her parents weren't as well off as mine and, although I didn't get much pocket money, I did get paid for the chores I did around the house. I hadn't thought it mattered, between friends.

I had something else to think about. Everyone in

24

our school had to sign up for some kind of sport, and you couldn't get out of it by playing in the orchestra or having speech and drama lessons or anything. I wasn't going to go swimming again, so what could I switch to, two weeks into the summer term?

Or was I being a coward and dropping out at the first setback? Perhaps I could switch to running. I was small and light, and perhaps I could train for track events. That would get me away from water, and that wouldn't be a bad thing, would it?

We filed out of the hall and along the corridors to our different classrooms. I saw Nicola's pony-tail of hair bobbing along ahead. She was busy talking to Kerry. Kerry was the one she'd said she was in love with.

'Watch it!' said a voice. I'd nearly walked into a half-open door. A capable hand steered me into the classroom and sat me down at a table near the back. Clemmie got out her books and thumped them on to the table.

'What's first period? Double maths? Open a window, someone, before I pass out. I always feel ill in maths lessons.'

I got out my books mechanically and stared out of the window. Nicola had found herself a seat next to Kerry and had never even looked my way. The maths teacher was late.

Clemmie tapped me on the arm. 'Wake up. I hoped you'd be in the pool for early practice this morning. You usually are, aren't you?'

I said, 'What?' and tried to think what she'd been saying. She looked me full in the eyes and smiled. It was a gentle smile.

The message came across loud and clear; Clemmie

25

liked me and wanted to be friends.

I was so grateful that I smiled back. 'Synchro?' I said, 'I'm giving it up.'

'They won't let you.'

'But I can't go on with it now!'

'Weren't you listening in assembly? H.H. said sport was sacrosanct, or something equally daft. He said everyone had got to stick to it and not give up, no matter how they felt about it. Good solid character-building stuff. Apparently some nerdish characters have been trying tennis one week and cricket the next and never settling down to anything. So we all have to stick to what we signed up for.'

'Straight up?' I asked. 'You're not having me on?'

'Straight up,' she said. 'Of course, Debbie might throw Nicola out of the club after what she did last night, but I doubt it. Our Debbie always tries to see the best in people, doesn't she? And besides, there's this Gala business coming up, and she'll need every single one of us for that.'

I didn't want Nicola to be thrown out. She was passionate about synchro, even though she had missed the last few early morning sessions. But I wanted out and, if what Clemmie said was true, how on earth was I going to manage?

3

The Break-up

'Psst!' Someone knocked against my elbow. I started and looked around. Where was I? Oh, in class, and it was the last lesson of the day.

A voice said, 'Perhaps Jan can tell us how an early Tudor cottage might have been constructed?'

The history teacher was staring at me. Everyone was staring at me, turning round and staring.

I blushed. I couldn't think of anything to say.

Clemmie twitched at my skirt. I glanced down. She had drawn something on the cover of her rough book.

My mind cleared. 'They used to bend two trees over till the tops touched and tie them together to make a sort of upside down 'U'-shaped framework. Then they filled in the gaps with bricks or whatever else was handy.'

'Very good. I thought you were asleep, but obviously you were taking it all in. Now, if they didn't have bricks, what other material might they have used . . . Nicola?'

There was a lot of sniggering when it became obvious that Nicola didn't know.

I knew because the parents had taken Chas and me on an outing to an open-air museum, and there'd been one of those early cottages there, showing how they were constructed. Really weird, but sensible, if you consider what they had to work with in those days.

I felt wretched about not being able to help Nicola. If only we'd been sitting next to one another, as usual! I looked sorrowfully at the back of Nicola's head. Her neck had gone a dull red, which meant she was furious at being caught out. Kerry, sitting beside her, was looking up at the ceiling. Obviously he didn't know enough to help Nicola.

The day dragged to a close. I watched Nicola walk out of the classroom without turning round to look at me.

Clemmie said, 'Well, shall I see you tomorrow for early practice in the pool?'

I shook myself back to the present. 'Thanks for helping me out, Clemmie. I went blank for a minute and your sketch was brilliant.'

'We aim to please.'

'But Clemmie, I don't honestly think I can carry on with synchro. I know H.H. said we must but, if I go to Debbie and tell her, perhaps she'll let me off.'

'I shouldn't think she would. There's only just about enough of us to do a decent show as it is. You know it takes ages to train a synchro swimmer. She won't want to lose either of you. I reckon she'd have thrown Nicola out last night, if she wasn't short of people.'

'I'll just have to convince her, then.'

We walked down the corridor to the staffroom together. I knocked on the door.

Debbie came to the door. Her eyes went from me to Clemmie and back. I thought, she knows why I've come, and her mind's made up to refuse me.

I did my best, but Debbie was shaking her head

before I had my request half-way out.

'I'm sorry, Jan, but I couldn't let you go even if the Head weren't so keen on everyone sticking to what they've signed up for. You know I'm short of good swimmers as it is.'

'But I'm not all that good . . .'

'You're just fine. All you need is a bit more confidence.'

Clemmie said, 'She can have some of mine—confidence, I mean.'

Debbie laughed. 'I agree it wouldn't do you any harm to be a little more careful, Clemmie. Now, Jan, it's not only that I can't break the rules. I don't like to see you and Nicola breaking up when you've been friends for so long. Didn't you two get together last night?'

'No, and I don't think it's any good trying to make up. If we both stay on the Squad, there'll be an awful atmosphere.'

'All the more reason for you to try to make up again. Now I've got to go, girls. See what you can do to sort it out, will you?'

She disappeared. The school buildings were eerily quiet around us, except for the orchestra tuning up in the distant music room.

Clemmie said, 'I'll walk home with you, if you like. I live down by the Common. I can either go down your road to the Common, or by the High Street. I usually go by the High Street, but I don't mind going your way today.'

I could have done with being alone, but I didn't want to rebuff Clemmie when she'd been so nice to me. We walked in silence out of the school and down the road.

I said, 'Don't you have a special friend, Clemmie?'

'Not really. I used to go around with some girls from my church when I was in Middle School, but then we moved over this side of town, and I don't see much of them now. I go around with Lisa quite a bit, but she's been away for a fortnight with a flu bug.'

'I've never gone around with anyone but Nicola,' I said. 'We always sat together, did everything together. It was her idea that I should do synchroswimming. I didn't want to.'

I thought about telling Clemmie why I'd signed up to do synchro, but it might sound like a whinge, and I couldn't bear it if Clemmie thought I was a whinger, too.

'I got into it by accident,' said Clemmie. 'I meant to sign up for athletics, but someone told me this stupid joke, and I was laughing so much I signed up on the wrong sheet of paper.'

'You're joking!'

'I'm not. The list for athletics was right next to the one for synchro. The athletics page was full, and I thought the one next to it was a continuation, and so I put my name down. Then I found out that I'd put myself down for synchro and I didn't know anything about it. I was going to back out, but I thought, well, maybe it's all part of the pattern, life's rich tapestry, God's plan for me, etcetera, and so I stuck it out.'

I was a little shocked. Knowing Clemmie, it was just the sort of stupid thing she would do.

'Do you like synchro?' I asked.

'Not much. It's too much like hard work, swimming. I mean, I knew how to swim already, after a fashion, but all that ballet leg and trying to be graceful, it's not easy when you weigh a ton and a half...'

'You don't! You're perfectly all right!'

'Not for swimming, I'm not. I'm the wrong shape, or weight or something. I suppose I could get better if I concentrated, but the others are all so much better at it than I am, so I tend to try for a bit and then give up and make a joke of it.'

We reached my house and paused by the gate.

'Well, thanks for everything,' I said, feeling awkward.

'No probs. Shall I see you in the pool early tomorrow?'

'Why do you bother going for early practice, if you hate it that much?'

'I don't hate it, exactly. I've signed on for it and I'll jolly well do it if I have to, but it's not easy to improve, working at it on your own.'

I nodded.

'You couldn't give me a bit of help, could you?' said Clemmie.

I stared at Clemmie, seeing not her eager smile but a stretch of dark water shadowed by willow trees. I could feel myself begin to choke.

'What is it?'

'Nothing. Maybe. I don't know.'

'See you tomorrow, then.'

'See you.'

Mum was back from her part-time job at the charity shop, but Dad hadn't come in yet. Chas and his friends were having a fight in the living room, to judge by the racket.

'Have you rinsed out your swimming things?' Mum yelled from the kitchen, hardly waiting for me to get in the door. She was throwing things into the chopping machine and had to shout above the noise.

'I didn't go for extra practice today.'

'Oh. Why not?' She didn't really want to know. She was just making conversation.

'I was a bit tired. I was thinking of switching to something else. Tennis, maybe. But H.H. said . . .'

'I wish you wouldn't use that nickname.'

She switched the machine into top gear and conversation became impossible. I fed the cat and emptied the dishwasher. Those were two of the jobs which I'd collected over the years. The cat's all right. Not really a sociable cat, more a misplaced ratter. We respect one another, and he never bites me as he sometimes does Chas. Of course, Chas does tend to tease him, which is stupid.

I'm enthusiastic about the dishwasher. If there's one thing I really hate, it's washing up by hand. I began putting the glasses on to their shelf.

The noise of the chopping machine died to a growl. Mum poured the raw mixture into a dish and put it in the microwave. 'Your father's going to be late, so we'll eat without him.'

I nodded, trying to get my jobs finished before she had time to ask any more questions or to mention Nicola. I didn't make it.

'Does Nicola want to do tennis, then?'

'We're not allowed to change sports, so it doesn't matter.'

'I thought she was getting on so well with synchro, hoping to take her first exam soon.'

I thought, not at this rate she won't. Not if she keeps missing practice. And I thought, Mum might ask sometimes how *I'm* getting on, and if *I'm* going to take my Grade One soon.

She was frowning at the microwave now, fiddling

with the controls. I put the last of the glasses up on the shelf and would have made my escape, but she stopped me.

'I met Nicola's mum in the supermarket. She asked what you were going to wear to some party or other this weekend. I wish you'd told me you were going to a party. She said she'd take you and Nicola, and I arranged to bring you both back.'

Complications. 'I haven't been asked to the party. It's no one I know very well. I think Nicola's going with a boy called Kerry.'

'With a boy? That will be news to Mrs Callender. I'd better give her a ring.'

She reached for the phone on the wall, and I got out of the kitchen, quick. Then I realized that I'd better be around in case there was any flak about Nicola stealing the money, so I stayed in the hall, pretending to fish my gloves out of my jacket.

I heard Mum get through to Mrs Callender and pass on the titbit about Nicola suddenly growing up and acquiring a boyfriend. They both thought it was funny and laughed about it a lot. I didn't think it was funny. Kerry was an absolute berk, and Nicola always used to say that she didn't even like him.

Then I realized that Nicola's going with Kerry to the party was a copper-bottomed, perfect excuse for her not hanging around with me so much. No questions were going to be asked about why we were no longer bosom pals. Love excused all.

I dragged my school bag upstairs to my room. I had never tried to work in the same room as Chas; that would have been asking for trouble. I sat at the table and put my head in my fists. I didn't normally indulge in bouts of self-pity, managing to grit my teeth and carry on regardless. But just for a moment I allowed myself to think how unfair life was.

It wasn't me who had stolen the money.

I'd always done what Nicola wanted, and she'd betrayed me.

She'd got off scot free, and got them all laughing at me and thinking me a real nerd. And now she was going to a party with a boyfriend, and I was left all alone.

Mum came into my room without knocking. I wish she wouldn't do that. She was looking all bright and cheerful. I guessed what was coming. She was going to try to cheer me up because Nicola had got a boyfriend and I hadn't. I clenched my teeth.

'Well, fancy that!' she said, fussing around the room, realigning the pictures on the wall, which didn't need it. 'Fancy little Nicola with a boyfriend. You girls do grow up so fast, nowadays. It seems only yesterday that you two were making sandcastles on the beach together ...

That was when we were six, and my family had taken Nicola away with us on holiday to the seaside.

' ... and now she's actually got herself a boyfriend! What's he like?'

I shrugged. 'All right, I suppose.'

'Now, you mustn't be jealous.'

'I'm not.' It was true. I wasn't jealous. If Nicola wanted to go off with a boy, if she'd changed that much ... She must have changed a lot, and I hadn't noticed it happening.

'That tone of voice tells me that you *are* jealous. Well, darling, I'm afraid it's all part of growing up ...'

'All part of life's rich tapestry ...' I thought of what Clemmie had said.

'What?'

'Nothing.'

That threw her for a bit. She folded some sweaters that had landed on the floor and packed them into my cupboard. 'I suppose you'll be asking for new clothes and earrings and wanting to wear lipstick and eye-shadow soon . . .'

I doodled on my scratch pad. Obviously she didn't know that Nicola had been wearing eye make-up for ages and had no less than four pairs of earrings. It's odd what parents don't notice when they don't want to know about it. Now if *I'd* turned up with pierced ears and great big hoops in them, World War Three would have broken out.

' . . . but there, I'm not going to push my little girl into growing up too soon, am I? Your father's always said you like to take your time about things, and I'm sure he's right. But little Nicola with a boyfriend . . . How about that? It seems only yesterday . . . I expect you're feeling a bit lonely, aren't you?'

I thought, little does she know!

I made some sort of noise in my throat which she must have taken for agreement, because she stooped down to give me a hug. Mum's not the kind that goes around touching people normally, and I was a bit taken aback.

'There, now,' she said, in a brisk voice, 'We mustn't let it get us down, must we?'

Oh no! I thought. Not another royal 'we'!

She said, 'Do you want to talk about it?'

This was so embarrassing! I could have died! I shook my head.

'Ah well, I don't suppose it'll be long before you get yourself a boyfriend, too. Supper's nearly ready, so don't get too deep in your books.'

She went downstairs and I let myself in for a bout of quiet screaming. There are times when you've just got to scream and shout and tear things up or you'll go mad. Only you've got to do it quietly, or they'll say, 'It's her age!' If you put your head under a pillow and lie on the bed and beat up the bedclothes, no one hears. Then you have to wash your face in cold water, so that they don't notice anything. Over the years, I've learned to scream very, very quietly. It's quite a useful talent. Saves you being carted off to the funny farm, anyway.

4

Someone Else's Problem

I was trying to finish a chapter of my English book while eating my breakfast. The front doorbell rang, and Chas skidded in from the hall to yell, 'It's for yoohoo!'

At once I thought it was Nicola, come to make up and walk to school with me. I grabbed a piece of toast to take with me.

'Who is it?' asked Dad, glancing up from the newspaper.

'Dunno,' said Chas. 'Someone from school.'

My stomach went down to the basement. So it wasn't Nicola. I didn't want that piece of toast, anyway.

Dad emerged from his paper. 'How many times have I told you to ask for people's names, when they call?' He went back into his paper.

Mum said I'd forgotten my swimming things, so she'd put them by my school bag in the hall to remind me.

It was Clemmie. She was kicking at a broken piece of pot in the porch. It's a big porch, and Mum keeps her bay trees in pots there. Chas had broken one of the pots the other day and there were bits still lying around. If I'd broken one, there'd have been no pocket money for weeks, but he'd just got a telling off.

I didn't know what to say to Clemmie. It was nice that she'd taken the trouble to call for me, but I didn't think we had anything in common. She didn't seem to have much to say, either, so we walked along the road in silence.

When we got to the main road, she led the way to the pool and I followed her because . . . I don't know why. Because she expected me to do so, I suppose.

Debbie lifted her hand to us and said hello as we went in. Di was in the changing room. She turned her back on us and I thought she'd taken against me because of Nicola. A fine start to the day.

Clemmie and I hurried to get ready. Not much time for warming up today. A few jump kicks, a bit of running on the spot, and then a neat drop into the water. Up to that point I hadn't panicked. The water was just water in a pool and I was thinking about something else. Then, at the moment I went under, I panicked. Keeping very still, I told myself that in a minute my head would break through the surface of the water, and all would be well. But the couple of seconds it took to surface seemed like a year.

Then I was up and bobbing around as usual. I took a few deep breaths to make sure and thought, this isn't worth it. I've got to find a way out of doing synchro. There must be a way, and I'm going to find it!

Clemmie was not her usual bouncy self. She bobbed around next to me and said, 'Four widths fast crawl, and then sculling, first forwards and then backwards, right?'

Looking at the pool, I saw only a weedy stretch of river, overhung by willows. I blinked, and it turned back into the pool. Some days I can push the river out of my mind quite easily. I said, 'OK.'

So we started in the usual way. Four widths to warm up, and then sculling, which is much slower . . . suddenly Clemmie did her oyster trick and I stopped, treading water.

She surfaced. No smiles, no jokes today. Debbie yelled at us to get to one side if we were going to muck about, so we climbed out of the pool and huddled into our towels to watch Debbie put one of the older girls through a complicated figure.

Clemmie said, 'You see, I'm no good at this. No good at all.' She was really depressed.

'Clemmie, what's wrong?'

'Dunno.'

'You must know. You're sculling away just fine, and then you suddenly give up and go under. Do you get cramp?'

'No.'

'Do you get tired?'

'No.'

I shrugged. She didn't have to tell me if she didn't want to.

Debbie came by us, and put a comforting hand on Clemmie's shoulder. 'Don't take any notice of Madam. I've told her to behave or else . . .' She walked on round the pool, calling out to Celia and Ruth to try again, they were splashing too much as they came out of their figure.

'What was that about?' I asked.

'Nothing,' said Clemmie, with a sort of restrained violence.

'Tell me!'

Clemmie turned her head away from me and then just as suddenly turned back. 'All right, if you must know, it's Di. She hates me. She waits till she thinks no one else can hear, and she says . . . things.'

'What sort of things?'

'You are slow, aren't you? About the colour of my skin.'

'What? But that's awful! How dare she!'

'Oh, Debbie tells her off whenever she catches her at it, but Di just bides her time and gets her knife in when no one else is near.' With a quiet despair, Clemmie added. 'It's not just that. I know I'm no good at synchro. I know I'm letting the rest of the team down. I can't help it. I do try, honest I do!'

'You and me both.' Suddenly it was easy to tell Clemmie my own problem. 'Did you know I was scared of water?'

'What! You? I don't believe it!'

Debbie turned on us and told us to hush.

'What was that?' Clemmie said, more quietly.

'I'm scared of drowning. Really scared. I'd never have done synchro on my own, but Nicola wanted to do it so badly, and she persuaded me it would be good for me, help me overcome my phobia. She promised to help me, always to practise alongside me. But now . . .'

'Ah-ha!' said Clemmie. 'Now I begin to see. Here's a how-de-do, Here's a pretty mess! Neat, don't you think? Neither of us can get out of it, and we both need help . . .'

' . . . so we help one another?'

'Definitely meant! Undeniably, magnificently neat! You've got to hand it to him, haven't you?'

I shifted about a bit. I wasn't quite sure what she was talking about, but it sounded, well, a bit naff, a bit 'religious'.

'Now look, Clemmie, if you mean Jesus and God and all that, well, I'm not really into it, you know.'

Her spirits were rising by the second. She gave me a brilliant smile. 'Am I embarrassing you? Well, I'm sorry about that. But it's true, you know. God is everywhere and he knows the answer to every problem including yours.'

I thought, oh yeah! But I let it pass, because I'd just had a brilliant idea about how to get out of doing synchro.

'Time!' Debbie blew her whistle, and we all scrambled off to change and get to school in time for assembly.

Clemmie bounced along beside me, talking all the time. I didn't listen much. I was thinking about my brilliant idea. That is, I thought about it till Nicola ran across the playground and into the school ahead of us.

Usually at this time Nicola was filling in her homework from mine. She's pretty bright, really. Only she doesn't have as much time to spend on homework as I do, since she has a paper round in the mornings and has to go to bed early because of it.

I wondered how she'd got on with her French. She hates French. I don't like it much either, but Dad had got me some cassettes to help me with my pronunciation and I'd lent them to her only last week.

Would she remember to give them back to me? It was strange how final our parting seemed to have become, so quickly. This morning at breakfast I would have been more than ready to make up our quarrel and pretend it had never happened. Now, I knew with a horrible, miserable certainty that this was never going to happen, that we were never going to be friends again.

Nicola sat by Kerry again, all morning.

Clemmie offered me some chocolate at lunchtime, but I didn't want it. I was off chocolate for good.

'What are you doing for the weekend?' Clemmie asked as we trailed out of the school gates together.

I checked in my stride. I hadn't thought about the weekend. Usually Nicola came round to me, or I went round to her, and we did things together. But Nicola was going to the famous party with Kerry.

The weekend stretched before me as a wilderness of wasted hours. ('A wilderness of wasted hours' sounded quite good. Maybe I could use it in a poem some time.)

'Dunno,' I said.

'I've got Lisa coming round—my friend that's had the bug, you remember? Well, she's better now and we're going to a jazz dance class. Like to come?'

I shook my head. 'Not my style.'

She said, 'OK, then,' and peeled off to make her way home by the High Street. I was sorry as soon as she'd gone. I'd never done jazz dancing, but it might have been a nice change from the usual ballet lessons which I'd given up only last term, and also it would have been something to fill in the time that weekend.

I went home and faced Mum doing her Understanding Mother bit. She had all sorts of suggestions for what the family might do for the weekend, like going to the Safari Park. Chas thought that was a brilliant idea, but then Mum remembered her car was going in for a service and Dad needed his for something, so we couldn't go anywhere by car. Chas sulked when she worked that one out, and he banged out of the room to stamp upstairs. He makes more noise going upstairs in his socks than I can by jumping up and down in my outdoor shoes. He really is a pain.

Then Mum suggested that we could go shopping for a new outfit for me. Chas was making so much noise by this time that she went out to shout at him, and I escaped to my room. It was quiet up there now that Chas had stopped stamping about.

I put on a tape and was just getting out my homework when I heard Mum climbing the stairs after me. I guessed she was going to come in to sit on my bed and have another of her embarrassing heart to heart talks. I simply couldn't stand it. I pretended to be busy, but it didn't work.

'Are you all right, darling?' she said.

'Fine, thanks. Got a lot of homework to do.'

'Oh. Well, just as long as you're all right.'

'I'm fine.'

'Is Nicola coming round this evening?'

'Shouldn't think so. I don't have to go around with her all the time, you know.'

'No, of course not. You're both growing up, it's bound to happen . . . Do you want to talk about it?'

'There's nothing to talk about.'

'No . . . well . . . Oh, I saw Mrs Callender in the Lane today and she was full of this Swimming Gala you're doing at the end of term. It sounds marvellous. I think she's rather hoping that you and Nicola will be doing some sort of duet together. I wish you'd told me. I didn't know anything about it.'

'Debbie did say something about a show at the end of term, but I don't think we're anywhere near good enough. I know I'm not.'

'Nonsense dear, of course you are. You must stand

up for yourself, you know. Don't let people put you down. You're far too inclined to let people put you down. But if you're doing a duet with Nicola, I don't suppose there's much chance of that.'

'Nothing's settled yet,' I said, thinking that this was yet another complication. All the more reason to carry out my Grand Plan.

'Well, as soon as you know, I'll put the date in the diary.' She drifted off and I chewed the end of my biro, waiting for her to get settled into making supper or whatever.

I needed peace and quiet for what I planned to do. I raced through some maths sums to pass the time. Chas would be going out soon, with a bit of luck. Ideally, I wanted Chas out of the house and Mum occupied downstairs.

My plan was simple. I was going to stage an accident and hurt myself, not very much but just enough to put me out of the squad.

The best place to stage an accident was on the stairs. I could jump or fall down the last few and pretend I'd come the whole way down. No one would know I hadn't. If I sprained an ankle, all well and good, because it would swell up and give me a perfect alibi. But if I didn't do much damage, then I must pretend that I'd pulled a muscle in my leg and limp a lot. Mum was dead keen on First Aid. She got out the bandages or the cough linctus at the slightest opportunity, quite often when it wasn't necessary.

I heard her yelling at Chas, and then I heard him crash-banging down the stairs. The front door slammed. A moment later, the TV was turned on in the livingroom, immediately under my bedroom. So the coast was clear. Chas was out and Mum was watching

TV. I could creep down the stairs till I was nearly at the bottom and then jump and lie there till she rushed out to comfort me.

I opened the door and stepped out on to the landing.

5

The Wrong Way Out

It was a dark day, with rain driving against the windows. I hovered on the landing. Should I put on the light? Better not. If I couldn't see properly, it would make my story all the more convincing.

From the top of the stairs I checked that Mum was in the living room. All was well; I could see the flicker of the TV through a crack around the living room door.

I was only two steps down and watching that crack of light when I felt the floor shift under me. I shrieked. I tried to stop myself falling by clutching at the bannister. My left arm snatched at the wood, but this only turned me slap into the banister. My arm was nearly wrenched out of its socket. There was no security for my feet. I took off into space.

I don't remember the last bit. I came to, lying with my head on the hall floor and my legs sprawling somewhere above me on the stairs.

Chas was gaping down at me. He seemed to be asking me something.

I tried to speak and couldn't.

'Don't move!' he said. At least, I think that's what he said. He ran away and came back with Mum's big coat to put over me.

I didn't want to move. I stared up at the ceiling in the hall, thinking angrily that this wasn't what I'd meant to happen, and that somewhere or other I was hurting a lot. Then the anger went, and I had to concentrate on just breathing in and out.

Chas' face swam back into sight. 'Don't move, whatever you do. Mum's just gone out to the shops for some veg. She'll be back in a minute.'

I worked it out. I had thought Chas was out and Mum was in, but it was the other way round.

I whispered, 'I fell ... something on stairs!'

Chas went red. 'One of my trainers. It must have fallen out of my bag. Mum yelled at me for being untidy, so I took my bag upstairs and it must have slipped out. But you should have seen it.'

I hadn't been looking. I thought about that, slowly. It was poetic justice. I had been planning to put myself out of action, and I had done just that. I couldn't think how I'd come to be so stupid! What on earth had got into me, to think of doing such a thing?

Chas crouched down beside me, looking scared.

He said, 'Shall I phone for an ambulance, or wait for Mum to get back?'

I didn't reply. My various hurts were calming down, except for my head and my left shoulder which was beginning to ache quite badly.

Chas was fidgeting. 'She ought to be back by now. Suppose she meets someone and starts gossiping. You know what she's like. There was a boy fell off the parallel bars at school and the games master said we mustn't move him ... and I haven't moved you ... and keep him warm ... Mum's coat's OK for that ... and just wait for the ambulance. I'd better ring them.'

I didn't reply. His reasoning seemed sound to me. He went to the phone, pushed buttons for 999 and asked for an ambulance. He told them I'd fallen down the stairs, that I hadn't been moved, and he'd covered me over. They seemed satisfied.

He came to sit on the bottom step of the stairs with me.

'Sorry, Jan,' he said.

'That's all right.' My voice wasn't quite my own, somehow. I wasn't really hurting now, except for my head, but I certainly didn't want to leap up and start square dancing. I closed my eyes and tried not to think about anything.

Time passed.

Maybe I dropped off to sleep.

I heard someone blowing their nose and opened my eyes a crack to see Chas sniffling into a tissue.

I tried to say, 'I'm quite all right,' but although I knew what I wanted to say, I couldn't get it out. I tried to smile at him, but he didn't seem to notice.

Then he got up and rushed out of sight. I heard voices. It was the ambulance men and Mum, who had arrived back home to the alarming sight of two paramedics going into her house.

They asked me where I hurt, and I couldn't even answer. I closed my eyes when they started to pick me up. It was easier to blot the scene out.

I'd always thought how exciting it must be to go off in an ambulance with the sirens going, but I didn't get much fun out of that particular ride. I opened my eyes once or twice, saw Mum's anxious face and went to sleep again.

What happened when I got to the hospital was not very nice, but of course they had to be sure that I hadn't done myself a permanent injury.

Wrenched muscles, scraped skin, and a spot of concussion. That was all. They kept me in overnight, to make sure the concussion wasn't going to develop, and then the doctor came round and told me I could go home.

'Nothing to worry about,' he said, 'bar you might have a headache now and then . . . keep checking with your G.P. . . . I hear you're a good little swimmer. Nothing like it for exercising the muscles. Splendid. Well done.'

I might have won a gold medal, the way he was patting me on the head. Or on the arm, rather. The arm that wasn't in a sling.

It seemed I couldn't do anything properly, not even get myself put out of action enough to stop swimming. I deserved every ache that I'd collected in my journey down the stairs.

The doctor said, 'I gather you have your little brother to thank for these bumps and bruises . . . that's quite a nice black eye he's given you, isn't it? . . . but never mind, you'll soon be able to get your own back on him, won't you?'

Mum came to fetch me in a taxi because her car was still in the garage for its service. She was torn between being angry with me for disrupting the household, and worrying about my injuries. And, as I learned later, she was furious with Chas for causing the accident.

I got out of the taxi and looked up at the house. The windows of the house looked blankly back at me. They knew my secret—what I'd planned to do, and that the accident wasn't all Chas' fault—but the house

49

wasn't on my side, or on Chas' side. It was just a house, somewhere to live in.

Mum bustled me indoors and installed me on the settee downstairs with the remote control for the TV to hand. No sign of Chas. She fussed a bit, asking what I'd like to eat and whether she should get me a video to amuse me. She said I'd probably be having visitors that afternoon, but that they weren't to stay long.

I said, 'Maybe I'll just close my eyes for a bit.'

She said 'Of course,' and bustled out, biting her lip. I was sorry I'd upset her.

I couldn't eat much lunch, and I went to sleep again straight afterwards.

I woke up to see Nicola sitting opposite me. She was chewing her lip and sitting on the edge of the seat.

I said, 'What are you doing here?' It was a bit of a shock, seeing her like that when I'd never expected to see her in my house again.

She sounded angry. 'Your mum rang my mum, and ordered me to come over.'

'I didn't ask for you, and I didn't say anything.'

'About what?' She was angry, perhaps with herself, and perhaps with me.

I couldn't see clearly out of one eye, and everything was hurting. I wished Nicola would go away.

'What about?' she repeated, loudly.

I closed my good eye. 'Don't shout. I haven't told her anything, about the money, or us not being friends any more, or anything.'

'*You* haven't told her anything! I like that! What do you think you *could* tell her? It was only a joke, but you turned it into something else, showing me up before everyone, making Debbie go on at me in front of everyone, and I only did it for fun!'

'OK, it was a joke,' I said, though I didn't believe her. It hadn't been a joke. It had been something deeper, or she wouldn't have reacted as she had. 'Forget it.'

'Forget it?' Her voice rose. 'How can I? With everyone looking at me all the time, and Debbie saying those awful things, and you going round like a dying duck in a thunderstorm, trying to get everyone to pity you . . .'

Mum walked in, looking annoyed but trying to smile because, after all, Nicola had always been one of her favourites. 'Something the matter? Nicola dear, a cup of tea, drink of Coke, a Penguin biscuit?'

'No thanks,' said Nicola, trying to be nice to my Mum while squinting her dislike at me. 'I only just popped in. Got to be going. Got to meet a friend, you know, the party.'

'Of course. Poor old Jan, she didn't half do herself an injury, didn't she? Doesn't feel much like anything today. I'm sure she'll feel more like herself tomorrow. Pop in again, whenever you like. You know you're always welcome.'

Nicola shot me a look labelled 'poison' and left. I closed my eyes again. It was all too much.

I could hear someone creeping across the room. The movement was so stealthy that I listened for a bit before trying to open my eye. It was Chas, peeping at me while tiptoeing across to the bookcase.

'I'm awake.'

'Oh.' He looked as if he expected me to bite, and then he made it to the bookcase. 'Just looking for the dictionary.'

'You can watch TV if you like. I really am awake now.'

'No can do. I've been grounded for a week, no going out in the evenings, no TV.'

'Oh, but . . .' I stopped. I couldn't say it had all been my fault, because then I'd have to explain why I'd been so stupid as to want to fall down the stairs. To be exact, I hadn't really wanted to fall, I'd just wanted to get out of doing synchro. What a muddle it all was. One thing was clear, Chas oughtn't to have to suffer for it.

I struggled to sit upright. I said, 'I'm sorry. It really wasn't your fault. I ought to have seen the trainer.'

'Mum said I might have killed you, and Dad said that if you'd broken something, he'd have given me such a thrashing as I'd never forget!'

I almost laughed at that. 'Well, you know he didn't mean it.'

'No,' Chas agreed, with a glimmer of a smile. 'No, I know he's a real soft touch, normally, but this wasn't normal, was it? I mean, it's quite true that I might have killed you.'

'No, not you, Chas. It was me being clumsy. I ought to have seen the shoe . . .'

'It was dark on the stairs. I nearly didn't spot it, either.'

'Look, shall I tell Mum it was partly my fault, and could she let you off . . .'

'No. I don't like being punished, but I got such a shock when I saw you lying there, I, well . . . I promised Mum I'd be a lot tidier in future, and never leave my trainers out for anyone to fall over again. Nor my school bag in the hall, or anything.'

'Don't overdo it.'

'What? Oh. No, I won't.' He grinned at me in his usual fashion and came to sit beside me on the settee. His weight made the cushions shift and set up a few hurts I'd not been noticing too much. He saw my face change and jumped up. 'I can't do a thing right, can I?'

'It's all right, honest . . . or it will be in a minute.'

'I'll fetch Mum.'

'No, don't.'

But he was off. Mum came fussing with drinks and aspirin and chivvied me up to bed. It was only when I reached the dark landing that I thought of Nicola who must have been preparing to go to her party just about then.

I tried to hope she'd enjoy it, but I'm not perfect, and I can't say I really meant it.

The next day my head was better but the rest of me wasn't. It was the bruises coming out. I hobbled downstairs with Mum clucking around me and, when Dad went off to watch Chas play football, I ended up in the living room, attempting to do my homework. Mum was really crowding me, with offers of hot-water bottles and cold drinks. I never have liked being fussed over.

I like to have music on when I'm doing homework, so Mum switched the TV on for background noise and went off to the kitchen, only popping back three times to ask if I wanted a window open, the cat in with me, and whether I would prefer baked or boiled potatoes for lunch.

I whizzed through my French, worrying a bit about the cassettes I'd lent Nicola. Something told me it wasn't going to be easy to get them back. I knew they'd cost a bomb and Dad had only got them because he thought they'd be useful for Chas as well, later on.

Then the programme changed, and there were people in church, singing. I was going to switch over when the words got through to me . . .

' . . . For those in peril on the sea!'

I sat there with my biro poised over my English homework, thinking about sailors on the sea in a storm, and what it must be like to be on a sinking ship. Did sailors not mind so much about drowning? I wondered. To me, it was the most awful death imaginable. If I'd got a choice, I suppose I'd say a heart attack would be best, or being in a plane that crashed. Something quick.

I'd seen bits of these church programmes before, in passing or before switching over to something else. Sometimes it seemed as if the words coming out of the people's mouths didn't mean much to the singers. But the way the people were singing this hymn struck me as different. They were singing 'For those in peril on the sea' as if the words really meant something to them.

Then this chap got up in the pulpit and again I nearly switched over, only Mum came in at that moment with a glass of Coca Cola for me, and she was humming the same tune. Of course, there's a miniature TV in the kitchen, so she doesn't have to miss any of her programmes while she's cooking.

'We used to sing that a lot, when I was a girl,' she said, putting another cushion behind me.

'You went to church when you were my age? I didn't know that.'

'There's lots of things you don't know, my girl. Yes, I used to go with your Grandad. He loved to sing. Not these modern hymns, but all the good old ones.' She went off singing, mock baritone, '...For those in peril on the sea.'

Well, stone the crows. I didn't remember us ever going to church as a family, though sometimes Dad took Chas to parade, because he's a Cub Scout and someone has to take him.

I never wanted to go to parade services when I was a Brownie, and anyway I dropped out of all that ages ago. I can't remember Mum ever going, not for anything. Yet here she was, saying that she used to go with Grandad. Grandma died ages ago, and Grandad only last year. We never got to see him much, though Mum used to go up now and then to visit. I was quite glad we didn't have to go to church on Sundays, because it seems such a waste of time at weekends.

I made to change channels but turned the sound up by mistake. This chap was saying something about doing things that you have to do with a will, doing them as well as you possibly can. Even when you'd rather be watching TV...

That got a laugh. I started to laugh, too, and then I realized he might have been saying that direct to *me*.

What he could have said was that as I'd got to do synchro-swimming anyway, I ought to do it as well as I possibly could.

I thought, fat chance.

Not to mention Clemmie relying on me.

I switched the TV off. That was enough of church stuff for one day.

Mum was *still* singing that hymn. I got back into

my English homework. Was it that girl in *Gone With the Wind* who said, 'I'll think about that tomorrow'? My feelings exactly.

6
Who's For Charity?

Dad dropped me off at the Leisure Centre early on Monday morning. I had some spectacular bruises and various muscles still ached, but otherwise I was mending fast. I didn't even flinch much when Mum said that she was sure swimming practice would loosen me up nicely and popped my costume and towel into my school bag.

It was strange to think that I'd been through all that agony over the weekend, and no one knew except Nicola; and I didn't suppose she'd been spreading the news about. Well, I'd done with all that. I couldn't think how I'd come to be so incredibly stupid. Enough of the self-pity and on with the job!

I went across to the pool and changed. I was glad to see Clemmie's scarlet anorak hanging on the peg by the door. There were a couple of older girls there, but they were talking to one another and didn't notice that I'd been in the wars.

I went out into the pool area and limbered up. Clemmie was in the water already, practising somersaults in a back tuck position. She was getting a good position, with her knees right up to her chin, but her toes weren't pointed, and she splashed a bit instead of doing it smoothly.

I dropped into the water and did a couple of widths of crawl. It wasn't a fast crawl, but it did seem to ease up the muscles.

Clemmie flipped over again and surfaced beside me. 'Hi! How am I doing?'

'Fine, except you forgot to point your toes.'

'I didn't.'

'You did.'

'Show me, then.'

I showed her. I've always been able to point my toes in the water. It comes from having had ballet lessons since I was four. I surfaced flat on my back in a back layout position.

She said, 'You splashed.'

'I didn't.'

'Yes, you did. Let's see who can splash the most.'

We grinned at one another. We knew we didn't dare. Debbie wasn't on duty today but Anoushka was, and she was even stricter than Debbie about not splashing or mucking about.

We worked on somersaults till the whistle blew, and we climbed out to shower and change.

Clemmie peered at me. 'What's the matter with your eye? I *thought* there was something wrong, but it's hard to tell when you're in the water.'

'I fell down the stairs. It rather messed up the weekend. Look.' I showed her some nice big bruises, and she was suitably impressed. 'How was *your* weekend?'

'Oh, good on the whole. The jazz dance was great. You really ought to come, some time.'

I heard myself say that I would, and I could have kicked myself. What did I want with jazz dance classes? But it made Clemmie happy. She promised that she and Lisa would pick me up on Saturday and take me there. Perhaps I'd go, perhaps not.

Later in the morning, walking through into the classroom, we came face to face with Nicola.

'Hi,' I said, without thinking.

She looked straight through me. 'Did you speak?' she asked, all toffee-nosed.

I could feel myself beginning to go red. 'Did you have a nice party?' Kerry wasn't with her. Her hair was all rat tails and her skin was spotty.

'Yes, it was marvellous, absolutely terriff. What a shame you couldn't come!'

She was overdoing the enthusiasm. Perhaps it hadn't been such a good party, after all. I said, 'I was laid up, remember?'

Now it was her turn to blush, because it was obvious she'd forgotten. She looked at my black eye and looked away again. She was going to walk off, when I thought that it was silly, us going on like this.

I put my hand on her arm, and said, 'Look, Nicola, there's no need for us to be like this.'

'Like what?' she asked, nose in the air.

I drew back. 'All right, if that's the way you want it.'

'Yes, that's the way I want it.'

'OK, OK. But there's just one thing. Could you let me have the French tapes back, if you've finished with them?'

'What tapes? I haven't got any of your tapes.'

'But Nicola, you have! My French tapes that Dad bought me!'

'I've said I haven't got any of your tapes, and if you say I have, then you're a liar!'

She flounced off into the classroom while I stood

there with my mouth open, staring after her.

'What was that all about?' asked Clemmie.

I shook my head. 'I just don't know what's got into her. She never used to be like this.'

'You lent her some tapes, and now she wants to hold on to them?'

'I suppose so.' I didn't want to talk about it. I scurried into the classroom with my head down and took a seat at the back. Clemmie followed and sat beside me. Her friend Lisa was by the window. She waved to Clemmie, who waved back. Nicola was sitting by Kerry again and talking to him as if nothing else mattered but bringing a smile to his lips.

The first lesson after registration was French. Clemmie looked something up in her dictionary, wrote busily for a while and then passed the paper over for me to see. She had conjugated the verb 'to splash' in French. I laughed out loud, which didn't amuse our teacher. She made me collect all the homework and, while I was doing so, I noticed that lying on the top of Kerry's school bag were two French language tapes with my name on.

I went back to my seat. Luckily the teacher was only going on about the absolute necessity of having French pen friends. We'd heard all that before, so I was able to do some quiet thinking. I noticed that there was a considerable amount of space between Nicola and Kerry. In fact, he was half turned to a girl on the next table, a red-head with a fixation about ponies and no interest whatever in boys. Kerry seemed more than a little interested in Miss Pony Rider, and not at all interested in Nicola.

Here was a turn-up for the books. Nicola had started off by saying that Kerry was an idiot, had gone on to swear mad, passionate love for him, and had been thrilled to go to the party with him. She must have lent him my tapes, pretending perhaps that I'd given and not lent them to her. Now he seemed to have lost interest in Nicola and was going after Miss Pony Rider. I could almost feel sorry for Nicola.

Well, not quite. Everything was over between us, I could see that. Even if she came crawling back, I wasn't going to kiss and make up. She had shown herself to be two-faced and a liar.

And if she tried to be rude to me again in public, then I'd let her know that I'd had it up to here and she could jolly well go and jump in the . . . river.

'Right!' said Debbie. 'Is everybody here? Yes? Well, I want a word before you go. You may have heard a rumour that we're doing a Swimming Gala at the end of term. It means a lot of extra work, but I think it will be worth it.'

'Are we really good enough?' asked Di, showing an uncharacteristic lack of confidence.

'Oh yes, I think so. Several of you older ones will do solos and duets, those of you who are taking exams will do their routines and there will be three or four big set pieces in which you will all take part. Obviously not everyone is up to doing Eiffel Towers and Herons . . .'

We all laughed at that. Only Anoushka and Ruth were capable of doing the really difficult figures.

' . . . but you can all scull and do a reasonable breast stroke with a glide, and the crawl . . .'

' . . . and somersaults . . .'

'*Most* of you can do a somersault properly, yes,' said Debbie. 'I want everyone to do something, however small. Those of you who are practising routines for exams must work on them really hard. Anoushka and Ruth, and Di and Celia, will do their duets, and I shall be working with them twice a week after school to form a quartet.

'But if anyone else would like to do something, either with a friend or as a solo item, I shall be delighted. From now on, I'm going to be here every morning before school and every afternoon after school to work with whoever can make it. On Wednesdays and Fridays in particular I want no excuses, because that's when we'll be putting the big numbers together.'

Everyone looked thoughtful but several, including Nicola, were smiling.

'Now,' said Debbie, distributing leaflets, 'Ruth, who's taking A level art, is going to do us some posters to go up in town, and I want you all to take one of these small leaflets home with you and give it to your parents. Put the date in your diary first thing. We're going to have a dress rehearsal the night before, so mark that up, too . . .'

'You mean, we can dress up—in the water?'

'Certainly you can. I've arranged some sponsorship for the costumes we're wearing in our big numbers, because they've got to match. But for the individual routines and for the duets, you can wear what costumes you like, and pretty hats or headdresses as well. But do remember that the costumes must not be transparent or fall off when you get into the water.'

We all laughed. There had been one girl—she left the term I started synchro—who had turned up in a brand-new bikini, dived in, and come up without her bottoms! I don't think she ever lived it down.

'What's this?' said Nicola, reading the leaflet. 'For the International Children's Fund? What's that when it's at home?'

'Precisely what it says. The International Children's Fund sends workers where they are needed, to help children in trouble.'

'I don't see why we should have to work so hard, just for a charity!'

Debbie looked hard at Nicola. 'It's like this, Nicola. Suppose you had a father who hated the sight of you and knocked you about whenever he came in at night...'

'Well, I don't!'

'That's your good fortune, isn't it? Others aren't so lucky. Suppose you were living in a town that was being bombed, crouching by day in a cellar and coming out at night only to scrounge for food and water...'

'Ouch!' said Anoushka, who had a cousin in the Middle East who'd been through just that.

'... or suppose there'd been no rain on your farm for months and months, and there was going to be no harvest, and your stomach was swollen with hunger...'

We were all quiet, now. We knew that these things happened, but they'd seemed very far away from us, living in cushy surroundings.

'And then,' said Debbie, 'there are the children who are born with terrible handicaps, unable perhaps even to lift bread to their mouths. And young people living rough. Shall I continue?'

We shook our heads.

Debbie said, 'The International Children's Fund

does what it can to help. It provides food for the starving, care for the handicapped, housing for the homeless. A seeing eye, and a hearing ear for those in trouble. So let's do this Gala for them, shall we? Let's sell as many tickets as we can, get all our friends and relations to come. Let's work really hard to make it all worthwhile. And then perhaps we'll sleep more easily at night, when we think of those without bed, or food, or parents, or health, or anything.'

She picked up a clipboard. 'Now, I have two duets and a quartet filled in, and of course Anoushka and Ruth will do solos. Celia and Di, solo routines, yes? Now what else would you like to do? Samantha, I thought you might...' The others crowded around her, wanting to put their names down, Nicola among them. I waited to hear what she thought she could do.

At last Debbie turned to her. 'Now Nicola, how do you feel about...?'

'I could do a solo, because I'm working towards my Grade One, aren't I? But I don't think I've got time to do all the extra work for a duet with anyone.' By 'anyone' she obviously meant me.

Debbie looked hard at Nicola but only said, 'All right, Nicola. Bring me some music, and I'll look at your routine.'

She went through all the other members of the squad, making notes, encouraging and suggesting routines and music. Clemmie and I signalled to one another with our eyebrows and began to collect our things together.

'Just a minute, you two!' Debbie stopped us just as we were leaving. 'I've got an idea for a duet for you.'

A duet? Us? We looked at one another and laughed. Clemmie screwed her finger into her forehead, and I nodded. Debbie was definitely off her rocker if she thought she could make anything out of us.

When there were just the two of us left, Debbie said, 'Well, now. I've been watching you two, and you seem to work well together. Which gave me an idea. How about a Pink Panther and Inspector Clouseau knock-about comedy act? Clemmie can splash about all she likes, and Jan will be quick and slippery in the water. You don't have to do anything spectacular by way of technique, just choreograph a chase, giving Clemmie plenty of room for her comedy act. What do you think?'

'Wowee!' said Clemmie. 'You mean, I really can splash about as much as I like? And dress up in a Sherlock Holmes hat and have a big magnifying glass slung round my neck ... and be funny?'

'Exactly,' said Debbie, smiling. 'How about it, Jan? You could wear a bright pink costume, with floppy ears and goggles. You would dive under Clemmie and do ballet legs and surface in unexpected places.'

'Yippee!' screamed Clemmie. 'Oh, do say you'll do it, Jan!'

Actually, I was almost as excited about it as she was. 'If I can wear goggles ...?'

'Of course,' said Debbie. 'I've got the music on tape, and I've some ideas how we can choreograph it already. But if you and Clemmie can get together this weekend and work out what figures and strokes you think you can do, that will help. Then we'll have to plot out your moves on graph paper, making sure you cover the whole of the pool.'

'I can't wait!' declared Clemmie. 'I can see it all! I flounder around, looking everywhere but in the right direction, and she comes up beneath me and tips me over . . .'

'You've got the right idea! Now off to home you go.'

Going home, listening to Clemmie burbling on about the routine, I wondered what Debbie had really wanted Nicola to do. It wouldn't have been Nicola's style to do a Pink Panther routine.

Clemmie said, 'This is going to be brilliant! Aren't you excited about it, Jan.' I said I was.

And I was, really. It pushed the fear way down below.

7

The Pink Panther Routine

By the time I got home, I felt more like going to bed than being bright and cheerful and doing my chores. I tried to keep a low profile, but Mum started frowning as soon as I dragged myself into the kitchen. She yelled for Chas to come and feed the cat and empty the dishwasher for me, and I was packed off into the livingroom to have a rest in peace and quiet. I didn't argue. It had been a long day and, though I was mending fast, every now and then I just had to have a Good Collapse.

I felt like a Victorian heroine, reclining on the cushions in front of the TV. Perhaps I would be like Elizabeth Barrett, who lay on her sofa for ten years till Robert Browning walked through the door and got her back on her feet. And I seem to remember that Florence Nightingale spent all her time being ill when she wasn't bossing everyone around in the Crimea . . . or was that one of those famous women explorers our history teacher was always talking about?

Chas came in, trying to be quiet. With him that meant throwing the door open till it rebounded into the cup and saucer he was carrying. Some unusual language was rapped out. He tipped a pool of spilt tea from the saucer back into the cup and handed it to me with a sigh of relief.

'Phew, this butlering lark isn't as easy as it looks. Mum says do you want some aspirin?'

'No, thanks. I'll be all right in a minute.'

'You don't *look* all right.'

Instead of departing for his usual evening pastimes, he trundled the pouffe across the room towards me, balancing it on the top of his trainers. I thought he wasn't going to make it, but he got to me in the end and sat down, breathing heavily.

I smiled at him. He really wasn't all that bad, as brothers go. And he *had* brought me a cuppa. If he hadn't wanted to, I bet Mum could have shouted at him for hours, and he'd have found excuses.

He lightened up. 'You really are going to be all right?'

'Feeling guilty?'

'Yep, sirree.'

We grinned at one another. 'I'm OK, honest.' I gulped some tea. It was nearly cold, but I wasn't going to complain about that. He'd done his best. No one's perfect.

He was rubbing his knees and rocking backwards and forwards. Something was undoubtedly up! I could ignore him, as I usually did. But he *had* brought me the tea, so I asked what was the matter.

'Nowt.' First he was a Yankee, and then a Northern lad, by gum.

'Tell!'

He screwed up his face and leaned back so far I thought he was going to fall off the pouffe. 'Well,' he said at last, 'I heard something today at school . . . had to punch him all round the playground . . . what an idiot!'

This was going to take some disentangling. 'Who's an idiot?'

'Tommy Callender.' Nicola's younger brother was a bit of a tearaway, suspected of petty thieving from the shops. Nicola tried to ignore him.

'What's he done now?'

'Said you'd given some money and some tapes to Nicola and then tried to say you'd only lent them.'

I felt sick.

He said, 'Don't look like that! I know it's not true . . .'

'No, it isn't true. I don't know what's got into Nicola.'

'I do. Her dad's got the push. Been made redundant. It happened some time ago but he didn't want anyone to know. Only, money's tight. Tommy's been nicking stuff from the corner shop every day this week. Silly so-and-so, he's bound to be caught. But when he started saying things about you, I thought it was too much, so I kicked him around a bit. I warned my gang to watch him, and if he puts one finger wrong, we'll have him. Right?'

Poor Nicola, I thought, why didn't she tell me? She might have trusted me. If I'd only known she was short of money, I could have lent her some. If Mum had known, what would she have done? But if Mr Callender didn't want it known . . . how very difficult!

Chas said, 'I reckon that Nicola's not much of a friend to you, letting Tommy spread that sort of thing around. And she's been seen smoking in the Town Centre of a Saturday with some older boys.'

I thought, Well, if she's got enough money to smoke, then . . .

Chas said, 'You're not friends with Nicola any

69

more, are you?'

'What makes you think that?'

'You'd have jumped down my throat and called me a liar, if there hadn't been trouble between you. Besides, the word is out that you're thick with Clemmie Hood now. I like her better than Nicola.'

I allowed myself to be sidetracked. 'Why?'

'Dunno. Because she's real. Straight up. I used to like Nicola, but lately, well . . .'

It felt like treachery, listening to Chas talking about Nicola like that, but I was just hurt enough to enjoy it, in a weird sort of way.

' . . . she might say one thing to your face, and another behind your back.'

I let the silence deepen. Chas crept out, knocking aside the pouffe and the empty cup and saucer I'd put on the floor. He'd meant to close the door behind him, but it sprang open again. I dozed off, only starting awake when Mum came in to see how I was doing.

'Mum, did you know Mr Callender had been made redundant?'

'I heard something about it today. I'm surprised at Nicola if she thinks that it would make any difference to the way we feel about her. Poor little thing. She must feel it. The school fees are so high, and there are all those little extras . . . I wonder if she can get a bursary—that's a kind of scholarship. Perhaps there's some clothes I can sort out for them, some things that you and Chas have finished with. Only, she's just that bit bigger than you . . .'

She went rabbiting on, and I thought about the money that had strayed from my purse into Nicola's just when Debbie had asked for the money for the new costumes. I wished I'd known! It must have seemed to Nicola that I'd been trying to buy her friendship by offering chocolate and hot drinks, and all the time the family was really short of cash!

Knowing what was wrong helped take away the awful sore feeling I'd been carrying around with me when I thought about Nicola. In a way, I wouldn't have minded being able to help her, even now. Though I didn't know how. Mum had the right idea, being practical, I suppose. But even so, it must be awful to be all right for money one minute and having to accept cast-off clothes the next.

Mum found the cup and saucer on the floor and was about to shout for Chas when I said, 'Oh, Mum, leave it. Chas is all right.'

'Yes,' she said, giving me a straight look. 'He is, and I'm glad you've woken up to the fact at last. You don't usually have a good word to say for him.'

'Don't I? Well, he can be a pain.'

'He surely can.' Mum kissed my forehead and went out. I was surprised. We weren't a 'touching' family, usually. Then I got my homework out and started on my Geography.

'What I think is,' said Clemmie, 'that we start our routine with me pacing around the deck, asking everyone if they've seen the Pink Panther. Then you sprint up from nowhere . . .'

' . . . from the plants by the entrance to the changing room . . .'

' . . . and push me into the pool. I come up splashing and threatening you, while you dance around on the deck. What sort of dance, do you think? Then when I go to climb out, you dive in and swim underwater till you come up behind me and tug my arm . . .'

'When does the music start? When I push you in?'

'We'll ask Debbie. I've made a list of the things I can do, like somersaults and so on.'

'I can't do anything really well.'

'You can swim quickly and neatly, and point your toes and do a lovely ballet leg. We can have me as the Inspector looking everywhere for you, and then you put one leg up out of the water and swish it about and I watch it, all puzzled like . . .'

' . . . and then I surface and waggle my ears at you, and go under again before you can get there!'

We sat back and laughed. It was going to be a good routine.

'Do I get out of the water, once I'm in?' asked Clemmie.

'Mm, not sure. *I* could, though. You could chase me, and I could get out and dance around the pool while you're still pretending to struggle out, and then I could jump in from the other side . . .'

'Tell you what!' said Clemmie. 'My Mum's really good at making costumes. How about we ask her to make your ears and my hat and magnifying glass!'

'Would she mind? I've asked my Mum to get me a shocking pink costume, and she said, "Shocking pink? Darling, don't you think a pale pink would be more becoming?"'

We laughed together. Clemmie said, 'She's right, of course. For every day, shocking pink would be too strong for you. But for the routine, you can wear make-up and *not* the sort that washes off in water.'

We were eating our packed lunches in the playground because it was such a lovely day. Nicola strolled past, arm in arm with a boy who didn't look anything like Kerry.

Clemmie said, 'Kerry seems to have gone off her. That's the Patel boy she's hanging on to now.'

'You heard that . . .'

'. . . her father's got the sack, yes. I suppose it explains what she's been going through. It doesn't make it right, but it helps me to understand . . .'

'My feelings exactly. Except that I wish she'd told me. I wish . . . we were such good friends, for such a long time.'

Clemmie was intent on the grass at her side. 'I've been praying about you and Nicola, you know.'

I wasn't sure what to say to this. 'Really?'

'Really. Yes, I pray quite a bit, off and on. When something comes up and hits me. I didn't know about Nicola till last night, when Lisa told me. But I've been praying about you and water ever since you told me.'

'Oh.' No one had ever prayed for me before. Ought I to say 'thank you'?

'Has it made any difference? I mean, I thought it was helping, because Debbie has got us going on this routine, and you don't seem nearly as worried about water as you were.'

'No, I'm not. I'm still scared underneath. But, yes, it is different, now. I can make myself think about other things when the water begins to change and look dangerous.'

I suppose one *ought* to say 'thank you'. But I wasn't absolutely certain sure that Clemmie's prayers had helped me. It was probably just a lucky coincidence that Debbie had come up with something which helped me overcome my problem. On the other hand, I didn't want to hurt Clemmie's feelings.

'Thanks,' I said, knowing it sounded awkward.

'Don't mensh! You really don't need to thank me,

you know. Thank Jesus.'

This was getting embarrassing. 'Oh, well, of course.'

Clemmie glimmered a smile at me. 'Now you're just being polite. You don't know what I'm talking about, do you? Tell you what, come to church with me some time, OK?'

'Sure.' I didn't mean it, and she knew I didn't. She rolled over in the sun and closed her eyes. I saw that Nicola was sitting by herself some way away. The Patel boy had vanished. No one was talking to Nicola.

I looked at Clemmie and thought how lucky I was to have her as a friend. Then I thought of all the trouble surrounding Nicola, and I felt I had to do something about it. We might not ever be really good friends again, but perhaps I could make things easier between us.

I walked over to her. She looked up all pleased when she heard someone coming. But when she saw who it was, she looked away.

I sat down beside her. 'Nicola, I just heard about your Dad. I'm so sorry.'

She hugged her knees and looked at the horizon.

'Why didn't you tell me? It might have helped.'

'How? How would Miss Prissy Rich Girl have helped her poor little friend, eh? By giving her lots of chocolate?'

'I suppose you're right to be angry. I didn't think. I'm sorry.'

'I suppose you're going to say you would have given me that money, if you'd known I couldn't afford to buy the costume.'

'Would that have been the wrong thing to do?'

'You have so much, and I haven't anything. Why

shouldn't you share your money with me?'

'If you'd only told me . . .'

'So that you could look down on me and patronize me like you're doing now?'

'I'm trying not to.'

'Oh, don't be so . . . humble! Next you'll be telling me to keep the French language tapes!'

'No, Dad bought them for Chas as well as for me, so I must have them back.'

'Then go get them, if you want them so much. I'm sure Kerry will be delighted to give them to the Rich Miss Wakeman . . . especially as he's just passed them on to his new girlfriend!'

'Oh, no!' I was getting angry.

'Now she's going to lose her temper, isn't she?'

'It would serve you right, if I did.'

'See if I care!' said Nicola and, getting to her feet, she flounced off.

I sat there, feeling really angry with her, till the bell went. I had to wake Clemmie up for the next lesson.

8

'We Need Publicity'

The weeds were dragging me down. I cried out, 'No!' and the bubbles broke out of my mouth and curved away upwards towards the light. My lungs were bursting. My head went red and black and ...

I woke, gasping.

It was some time since I'd had the nightmare as badly as that. I sat up in bed with the light from the street lamp cutting across the duvet. I had cramp in my leg. I eased out of bed and stretched and kneaded till the pain was gone.

Then back into bed. I was cold now.

The water had been cold then too. It had been a lovely warm day, up above.

Mum knew I'd had the nightmare at breakfast by the darkness under my eyes.

'Why didn't you wake me?'

I just shook my head. What was the point? I shouldered my bag and left the house, but Dad caught me up in the drive and said he'd drop us both off at school, since he was going that way.

Chas got into the front as usual and made screeching noises as if the car were going round a bend on two wheels at eighty. He's quite good at it. Dad didn't attempt to talk through Chas' interpretation of a nightmare car ride but, after he'd dropped Chas off at the Middle School entrance, he drew into a lay-by and stopped.

'I'm a bit worried about you, you know, Puss.' He very rarely called me 'Puss'.

I smiled to show I appreciated he was trying to help. 'You won't knock yourself out doing the pre-school swimming practice today, will you?'

I shook my head. It was our official swimming lesson that day and, since I'd been to all the other practices and lessons, it probably wouldn't matter if I didn't turn up to the early practice for once.

Dad fingered his chin, running his thumbnail down the jawline one side, and then up the other. He always does that when he's stumped, like when he's doing the crossword, or his income tax return.

'Your mother thinks you're really getting over your old problem. You are better, aren't you?'

I nodded. I knew how this conversation went. In a moment he'd repeat the question to make sure I was OK, and then we'd leave the subject.

He twisted right round to face me. 'Because if you're not, then we could perhaps have a check-up with the doc, couldn't we?'

I shook my head. Mum always said I didn't need doctors poking around inside my head, and I was sure she was right.

'Well, if you're quite sure . . .'

I nodded and got out of the car. He waved to me and drove off into the traffic. It was nice of him to bother.

I took a misstep and stumbled. There'd been a strange lighting effect on the grass, and for a moment it had looked just like a pool of deep, weedy water. It's odd how your mind can trick you like that.

Debbie checked the last of us off on her list. She'd worked us hard and we were all tired, lazily getting changed back into our outdoor clothing.

'Now there's only one thing,' she said, frowning at her list. 'The tickets aren't going very well. Also we need backstage staff, lighting equipment, everything. One of the problems is that the members of the club are drawn from different schools, so I can't go to any one headteacher and ask for help.

'I've tapped the usual resources at the Town Hall for money for costumes and help with printing programmes, and they've done as much as they can. So now it's up to us, each one of us. Does anybody know anyone who can act as steward, for instance? But the main problem at the moment is that the ticket sales are not going fast enough. I think we need some publicity to get the idea of the Gala across. Any ideas?'

Anoushka said, 'A spot on TV?'

We all laughed to think that we could ever be on TV.

'Not a bad idea, though,' said Debbie. 'Work through the media, local radio perhaps. Local newspapers. Stick up adverts in all the local shops, the libraries, Town Hall and so on. I'll get some more of the posters run off, if some of you will volunteer to get them stuck up in shop windows and so on. Now Ruth, could you ask your head of department if he could help us with one or two props that we need for the gala?'

'I don't know.' Ruth looked doubtful. 'I mean, they're always so busy with course work and that.

78

I could try, I suppose.'

'Do your best. And is there anyone doing craft, needlework, that sort of thing? Samantha, bless you. I'll speak to you afterwards. And has anyone a contact in the home economics field? Or a parent who can organize some catering for us? It would be wonderful if we could get a buffet together, for the interval.'

No one volunteered.

'How about someone to put up some stage-type lighting?' asked Debbie, trying to keep cheerful but sounding a little desperate.

Anoushka perked up at that. 'I know, I'll ask the head of Languages at our school. He loves fiddling around with lighting and is always trying out new things for the drama productions. But I'm not good at explaining what we want. Could you do that?'

'I can see I'm not going to eat or sleep much till this is over. Yes, Anoushka, of course I'll meet him. Now what about the media? One of my friends works for the local paper, and I'll see if he'll give us a couple of paragraphs of background. We should also be able to get a mention in their Diary section. Anything else?'

'Radio,' said Celia, laughing. 'Who's going to tackle radio?'

'You may laugh,' said Debbie, 'but local radio's worth a try. They could give our Gala a boost by mentioning it on the air, and since it's for charity, and it's just that much out of the ordinary, we might even get an interview. I'll ring them and find out.'

I put up my hand. 'Please, I don't think many people in our school know what we're doing, and why. I mean, they think the Gala's just like any other end of term show, and they don't understand what the charity does. Do you think H.H.—I mean, the

Head—could tell them about it and ask them to help us and to get their parents to come?'

'We're always doing sponsored walks and silences for charity at our school,' grumbled Di, who went to the Convent. 'They think it's just one more call on their pockets. What's so different about this one?'

'Have you told them it's all about helping children in trouble.'

'Who? Me?' said Di, looking shocked.

'Don't you think it would come better from you? I do. We're asking for help for children, so who better than one of you, who understands the problem, to make the appeal! Ask your head of year if you can do it at assembly.'

'So who is doing it for our school?' asked Nicola.

There was silence. Clemmie pulled a face, and Nicola scowled. No one wanted to do it, that was clear. It was a scary idea, to have to stand up in front of the whole school and speak. I didn't envy whoever got stuck with it.

'I vote Jan does it,' said Nicola. She wasn't looking at me. 'Her mum works in a charity shop, and they always have a box in their hall for people to drop money into. And she's so little that everyone will feel sorry for her.'

'I don't know about that,' said Debbie. 'But Jan does have a nice clear speaking voice. I think she'd do it very well. OK, Jan?'

I froze.

Clemmie was laughing. 'I thought you might ask me, and I know I'd muck it up!'

They were all laughing now. Except me. I tried to voice a protest and failed. How could Nicola do this to me? She *knew* how shy I was. She was rushing off

80

now. Perhaps the others thought it had been her way of making up the quarrel between us.

I must speak to Debbie and tell her I couldn't do it. I rushed into my outdoor things. I was last, as usual.

I said, 'Debbie, I honestly don't think I can ...'

She pushed me out of the door ahead of her. 'I know, Jan. *You* don't think you can do it, but you see, everyone else thinks that you can. I watched you when you had a bit part in your form's Christmas play. You looked sick with nerves before you came on, but you went through your part very nicely indeed. I'd like you to try. Go home and write out what you think you ought to say. Write it out very clearly, and show it to me. Then all you have to do on the day is to read it out, slowly. I think you can manage that, can't you?'

I wanted to say that I couldn't, to run away, anything to escape. Instead, I nodded.

How ever did I get to be so stupid!

Clemmie was waiting for me outside. She was swinging her bag in great arcs, narrowly missing passers-by, who looked at her in a disapproving way. Clemmie didn't care. She was enjoying herself.

'Listen, you promised to come to jazz dance tomorrow ...'

'I said I might.'

'Well, why not? Do you good, loosen up the muscles. I could ask the teacher to show you what steps to use when you're the Panther, dancing around on the deck.'

I nodded. That was a good idea. 'All right.'

'Shopping afterwards? I've got five pounds. And something at MacDonald's for lunch?'

'I'll have to ask Mum.'

'Sure. Give me a ring. I'll write the number down for you.'

I resigned myself. Clemmie was rather like a perpetual motion machine. I might as well get it over with.

'Stay the night, if you like,' she said, casually. 'Bring your things, anyway. We're having a barbecue with next door. We always have one at midsummer. We throw the two gardens into one and invite all the neighbours and have lots of food. It'll be good.'

I didn't promise anything and I was careful not to sound as if I wanted to go to the party when I spoke to Mum. Actually I wasn't all that sure that I did want to go. It sounded, well, a bit noisy. Like Chas on the go for twenty-four hours a day. Wearing. I do like to be by myself, to be quiet now and then. But Mum was surprisingly enthusiastic, especially when Mrs Hood rang through to introduce herself properly and confirm Clemmie's invitation.

I saw Mum looking at me anxiously, and I knew she wanted me to go, because of Nicola and me no longer being friends. So it was all arranged that Mum would drop my bag over to the Hood's on Saturday morning, and I'd stay with them till Sunday evening. That suited Mum because then she and Dad could take Chas to some Air Show or other that I wouldn't have much liked, anyway.

By Friday evening, I was sorry I'd said I'd go. I was tired by the end of the week, and there was a lot of homework to do. I felt draggingly worried about the Gala and swimming and pure panic about standing up at assembly to talk about it. I sat on my bed and roughed out some sort of appeal to give at assembly, but it was hopeless, the words just wouldn't flow.

I was afraid I'd get the nightmare again that night. I'd noticed that it usually returned when I was overtired.

I woke in the usual way. Fighting for breath. My leg hurting.

If I could have got out of the weekend arrangements, I would have done so, but it meant disappointing too many people, especially Chas. I couldn't disappoint Chas, when I'd got him into so much trouble before.

So Mum dropped me and my bag off at the Hood's house, where Clemmie and Lisa were already waiting, hopping about, to drag me off to their jazz dance class.

Everyone at the dance class was wearing leotards and danced in bare feet, so I wore my new shocking pink swimming costume, to get some wear out of it before the Gala. Madam was a hoot: frizzy blonde hair and so many layers of clothing on, you wondered how she could even bend her knees. But when she got going, off came the layers, up went the decibels in her voice, and the class really took off.

I found a place in the back row and tried to copy what Clemmie and Lisa were doing in front of me. They were pretty good, I must say. Lisa, particularly. She had the sort of slender body that didn't seem to have any bones in it when she moved.

We did some basic exercises and then danced around to different rhythms following a sequence of steps. I was really involved, really enjoying myself, when suddenly I realized what music was coming out of the tape recorder. It was the Pink Panther theme!

I lost concentration for a moment and got shouted at by Madam. Clemmie and Lisa grinned at me over their shoulders and I realized they'd known Madam often used that music. They'd brought me along specially! I grinned back. And started to concentrate extra hard. Ta rah, ta rah, ta ra, ta ra, ta ra, ta ra, ta *rah*, de de diddle de *dah* . . .

I watched Lisa as if my life depended on it. I'd have to ask her if she would go through the steps with me later, so that I could get them by heart.

'Watch *me*, not Lisa!' cried Madam. She waved me to a place between Lisa and Clemmie, so that I could see exactly what she was doing. She was just great! Maybe I'd join her class for good.

When it was all over, we sat or lay around, breathing deeply.

'Good, wasn't it?' said Clemmie.

I nodded. 'Lisa, I wish you were in the synchro squad. You'd be just brilliant.'

Lisa shook her head. 'I'm aiming for a place at ballet school.' I said I was sure she'd get in, and I meant it, too.

We went off through the Saturday market in the centre of town. We looked at all the fashions and the make-up, although none of us was into make-up except on stage. It was good just to potter, knowing we had a little money to spend if we did want to. I looked at the chocolate and thought, I could get some of that for Nicola, and remembered, and turned away. I was 'off' chocolate, myself.

Lunch was all right, too. We got a table to ourselves right at the back at MacDonald's under a speaker and sang along with the hits. Then I saw Nicola drifting past in the street, looking as if she didn't care what happened to her. I couldn't get out and chase after her, not from where I was, sitting between the other two right at the back of the room. I knew it wouldn't do any good, either. She didn't want me any more.

'Who's that? Oh. Nicola,' said Lisa, in a non-committal tone.

'Poor thing,' said Clemmie.

'Why do you say that?' asked Lisa. 'Hasn't she been a right pain recently? I know about her father and all that, but she needn't take it out on the rest of us.'

'I think she hurts inside,' said Clemmie, slurping up the last of her Coca Cola and then burping.

'Oh honestly, Clemmie!' said Lisa, giggling.

'Wow, sorry,' said Clemmie. 'But I mean it, about Nicola. What do you think, Jan?'

'Yes, I suppose you're right.' I had some difficulty talking about Nicola. It still felt as if it was betraying her to talk about her behind her back. But Clemmie's concern was real and I wanted to explain Nicola to Lisa if I could. 'I do think she's hurting inside, but when I've tried to talk to her, she just...'

'...bites your head off?' said Lisa, grinning.

Clemmie wagged her finger at us. 'A spot of prayer works wonders. I have been praying for her, but two spots are better than one, and three are better than two.'

Lisa winked at me. 'Now she's going to ask us both to pray for Nicola as well.'

'Mm,' I said, not wanting to be pushed into doing something I didn't really believe in.

Clemmie screamed, 'Look at the time! I promised Mum we'd be home before half past to help her get ready for the party!'

9

What a Party!

The Hoods' garden was huge, far larger than ours.
The house was a rambling affair with rooms built out
over the double garage, plus an extension at the back.
The front garden was ordinary, with a neat belt of
shrubs around the driveway, but at the back the
ground sloped away over a lawn, down past a play
area with a double swing and climbing-frame, to a
patio in front of a bank of rhododendron bushes.

Mrs Hood asked Clemmie, Lisa and me to carry
some special torches down to the bottom of the
garden. They weren't torches with batteries in
them, but wax sticks about a metre long, which you
stuck in the ground. Once lit, they burned for hours.
We each took six. They weighed a lot.

Some men were setting up a barbecue under a sort
of open-sided tent near the house. Further down,
fairy lights were being tested around the patio. I
wondered why they wanted the special torches as
well, but Clemmie waved us on to a path through
the bushes, and beyond.

There was a small vegetable garden beyond the
bushes and beyond that ...

I stopped short, and Lisa cannoned into me.

'Watch it!'

Clemmie grinned. 'It usually takes people like that when they first see it. A bit of all right, isn't it?'

We were standing at the head of another sloping lawn, which led down to a wide-spreading, shallow stream. The stream curled away to left and right through neighbouring gardens. Willows dangled languid leaves across the surface of the water on the opposite bank. The sluggish run of the current gave me a queasy feeling.

'It floods sometimes,' said Clemmie, 'and then we're not allowed down here, because it gets so muddy. And because of the kids. Mum didn't want to buy this house because of the water, but Dad put up a fence and that's stopped them—so far.'

I looked around in bewilderment. I couldn't see any fence.

'It's been taken down for the party,' explained Clemmie, pointing to where some people were stacking sections of fencing. 'That's the people from across the road who've come in to help. Everyone comes to the party, so they all help.'

A patch of rough grass ran across the bottom of the garden, and where the lawn met this rough grass was a series of wooden posts to which the fence had been attached. Someone was already mowing the rough grass to match the rest of the lawn. The wooden posts supported rambler roses, throwing pink and red sprays of blossom high and wide.

Mr Hood came down from the house with a barrowload of garden chairs and said he was going to make sure the roses were all securely tied to the posts so that they didn't scratch anyone.

Clemmie said, 'We always have our party when the roses are out. It makes it more fun that way.'

I didn't like the look of the water. The current stirred the weeds in a gentle rippling movement. I knew what it would feel like to get caught in them.

Two of the neighbours moved on to take down more sections of fencing, this time between the Hoods' and the neighbour's garden.

'That's the golf course on the other side of the stream,' said Clemmie. 'Sometimes we find golf balls in our garden. We take them up to the club house and they give us something for them. And on our right, joining with us for the party, is our Uncle John's garden. He's lived there man and boy for yonks. He knew Dad at University, and that's how we came to live here. We were up north before. But I like this place better and so do the Brats.'

'The Brats' were Clemmie's younger brothers, all four of them. They all looked exactly alike, except that they went down in height from eight to two years of age. Two of them were 'helping' the neighbours stack fencing.

'If Mum catches them down here, they'll get What For!' said Clemmie. 'She's got this nightmare about one of us drowning. But I suppose they'll hardly come to any harm with Dad and everyone here. At the party there'll be plenty of people about, and the fencing goes back up tomorrow afternoon, so we'll just have to keep them out of harm's way tomorrow morning.'

I felt chilled by the thought of all those dangerous minutes between now and Sunday afternoon, but I didn't say anything. I helped stick the torches into the ground at intervals all along the verge of the stream. Then we ran up the garden to help bring down garden chairs. Men were setting up speakers for music by that time, and everyone was rushing around, saying they'd never be ready on time.

Long trestle tables were being set up on the patio. We three girls carried out great bowls of salads and enormous dishes of sweet things, covered with cling-film. I carted plates and napkins until I was dizzy.

One of Clemmie's brothers—I think he was the smallest, though I can't be entirely sure—decided that I was the only safe haven in a shifting world, and after a while I had to carry him around on one hip. He was gorgeous, all sweet and sticky. I almost wished we could have another baby in the family, if we could get one like Roop (short for Rupert).

At last we were sent up to rest and change for the party. Roop fell asleep on the bed in the room Lisa and I were to share with Clemmie. I didn't have the heart to disturb him. I wore my black leggings with a lilac and white top while Clemmie and Lisa wore colourful leggings with black tops. We discussed my borrowing some of Clemmie's things so that we could all look alike, but they just didn't fit. We laughed a lot.

I really enjoyed that party. We three had to look after the children of other guests and show them around and see they got enough food. At one time I think there were eighteen of us all under the age of fifteen. We stuck together nearly all the time.

We danced on the patio for a while. Then we wandered off down to the stream where most of the guests were sitting, and through the gap into the garden next door. That garden was quite different from the Hoods'. There weren't any play areas nor was there a patio, but they had a paved rose garden which was marvellous for playing tag. They'd set up a bar in a summer-house, and there were lots of fruity drinks with ice in them for us. Then—highlight of the evening—we were allowed to light the special wax torches with long tapers.

Everybody went Ooh! when we lit the torches. Sticking in the ground like that, they looked much better than the fairy lights around the patio. We three were all tired by then and got into a huddle on a big sun-lounger with Roop, who had gone to sleep again, and one of the other toddlers whose name I didn't know. Lisa and one of the boys went back to the dancing, but I don't know how they'd got the energy.

Mrs Hood found us and sent us off to bed eventually. Clemmie carried Roop up. Clemmie's Aunt Martha took him off us and put him to bed.

Lisa was supposed to sleep on a camp bed, but she said, 'Oh, I'm bushed!' and fell backwards on to my bed, and that was her, asleep! I tried to climb into the sleeping-bag on the camp bed, and it tipped me on to the floor, so I giggled a bit and said I'd sleep there.

Clemmie called me to the window to look out over the garden. From her room you could look right down over the slope and the bushes and over to the lights beckoning around the stream. The music was still playing on the patio, softened by distance. It looked so beautiful it made me want to cry.

Then I crawled into the sleeping-bag on the floor and that was it. Lovely sleep. Just lovely.

In the morning we all felt tired, but terribly hungry. I don't know why we felt so hungry, because we'd eaten quite a bit the night before.

The house was hushed with sleep, except for where the Brats were bumping around in the play room, with the TV turned on full blast. We got them quiet and properly dressed, and then Clemmie said she'd be cook, so we went into the kitchen and got out cereal packets and milk and bread and jam. Lisa found a plateful of chicken drumsticks in the fridge, left over from the party, and we ate those as well.

Clemmie's parents and aunt came down, yawning, and said, wasn't it a lovely party, but what a pity about the rain. I hadn't heard any rain, but apparently there'd been a cloudburst about midnight, which had stopped the party in its tracks.

I looked out, and everything did look lovely and clean. After breakfast we tidied things up. Then Lisa's parents called to collect her, and the rest of us piled into cars and drove off to church. Roop sat on my knee and they joked that he'd expect to go home with me that night.

I hadn't realized until then that we'd be going to church, but I didn't mind. I was feeling too good to worry about anything. Roop was such a sweetie I liked his sitting on my lap, although I did draw the line at wiping his nose when he sneezed. (Luckily Clemmie got some tissues from her mum and coped.)

I thought that we'd be going to the sort of church you see on the TV, like the one where they'd been singing 'For those in peril on the sea'. Sort of mid-Victorian-mock-Gothic.

Our history teacher had told us the Victorians had a passion for tearing churches apart in the name of progress and restoration. What he seemed to mean was that the Victorians stopped them falling down and put in central heating, neither of which seemed to me to be the crime of the century. The Victorians also took the box pews out and put in the kind of seating you see on the TV programmes. I did think that was a shame. It must have been nice to snuggle down inside a box pew, because it would keep all the draughts out.

This church wasn't like that at all. For a start, it was more like a school hall to look at than anything else, and inside there was a lot of thick blue carpeting, and people putting out stacking chairs. There didn't seem to be an organ or even a piano, but on a raised dais at the far end they were fiddling around with a drum kit and a synthesizer.

There was a table on the dais, but it didn't look much like the usual kind of altar. At one side they'd fixed up a giant screen with an overhead projector. All very informal, and not a speck of gold plate or any pretty robes to be seen.

What's more, no one was sitting in a chair staring straight ahead as they do on the TV. Everyone was hugging and kissing and talking just like at the party the night before. Weird.

The Brats—except for Roop—went off to play with some toys in a space at the side. Mrs Hood felt Roop's forehead and wondered if he was going down with a fever.

I got worried about him then, but Clemmie said he sometimes clung to her for a couple of days at a time, just getting a fit of the lonesomes. It all went back to when he was a tiny tot and got lost in a supermarket. He wasn't found for ages. He'd been 'clingy' ever since, and they said not to take any notice. So I said I didn't mind being his latest heart-throb and everyone laughed and said that with my long eyelashes, I wouldn't need to worry about collecting heart-throbs!

A bit embarrassing that, because we don't talk about looks in our family.

Then somehow we were all in our seats, in an

informal semi-circle, with more and more people being fitted in. Some man came in dressed in a big sweater and jeans, just like Dad at home at the weekends. This man appeared to be in charge, for he gave us a big welcome and started the singing.

The song was easy to pick up, because the drummer gave us a good beat, and the keyboard player really knew his business. It was the sort of song which gave you a nice warm feeling, praising God for everything he had given us. I soon realized there were a lot of things he'd given us that I'd taken for granted before. What I mean is, till it's pointed out to you, you tend to forget that human beings can't make things as complicated as flowers or trees. They sang quite a few of those songs, really getting into the spirit of things, and I joined in when I had picked up the tunes.

A lot of the people, including Clemmie, were standing with their eyes closed and their hands raised, palms upwards. One or two of them were swaying a bit in time with the music.

I was holding Roop, who was trying to go to sleep again, so I sat down and cuddled him. He *was* a bit of a weight to carry for long. No one minded that I sat down. There were some older people sitting down, too. A couple were in wheelchairs. But they all looked ... well, 'serene' I suppose is the best word.

Then a woman got up and led us in prayer. I can't remember now what she was praying about, but it felt just right. It seemed other people thought what she said was good, too, because they began to murmur agreement with her. They didn't wait for the end and say 'Amen' as they do on the TV. They just came right out and agreed with her. I rather liked that. 'Amen' is such a 'finishing' sort of word.

The next bit was just amazing. A woman came forward holding an airmail letter. It was from her son, and he had gone to some awful trouble spot to try to help the poor people there. They had next to no supplies and were under fire, even in the hospital. He knew he might not make it home again, and he had written to his mum to say that he was all right, because he knew that he was not alone; even though he might have to pass through death's dark valley, he knew that he was safe in Jesus' hands. He believed that Jesus went with him when he tended the wounded, and when he fed a starving child.

I wondered if the man worked for the International Children's Fund. It sounded as if he might.

Then something even more strange happened. I looked up and saw some letters on the wall above the musicians. I don't know why I hadn't noticed them before. The letters said: 'Living Waters'.

10
In Deep Water

The words hit me as if I'd been punched in the midriff. I could feel myself going 'Oof!' I didn't know what it meant, exactly, except that I was sure it had a special message for me, if I could only work it out.

The man who'd welcomed us got up to read from the Bible. It was as if he knew all about my problem and was there to help solve it. For the Bible reading could have been just for me. The part that really hit me was: 'Fear not... when you pass through the waters I will be with you; and through the rivers, they will not overwhelm you.'

I don't remember much about the rest of the morning. I know I stood up and sang with the rest and listened while they talked about Jesus and what he had done for them. Later on, and in fact for months after, I'd remember snatches of what we sang, and what was said. At the time, it was just a blur.

Inside, thoughts were churning around in my head. It was clear they were talking about something real, a love and a belief in God's love that changed them. Love. That was one of the words that they talked and sang about. But not just your ordinary, everyday love. This love was so great that it was everywhere, even in the darkest places and in the deepest water. God took away all their fears. I wondered if he could take away mine, too.

I was so tired when the service ended that I simply smiled and said it was lovely when they asked me if I'd enjoyed myself. We all piled back into the big car, with Roop crawling into my lap to sleep again, and drove off back to the Hoods'. I said Roop seemed a little warm, and someone felt his forehead and said they'd take his temperature when we got home.

For lunch we laid out everything that was left over from the party, took a plateful and wandered into the garden to eat it. The people came in from next door to talk over the party and say what a pity it had been cut short by the rain. The grown-ups drifted back into the kitchen to make coffee. It was a beautiful day, washed clean and blue. The sky was so clear, you could look up for miles.

Suddenly I missed Roop.

The moment I realized he wasn't tagging at my heels, I knew something awful had happened. I raced into the kitchen to warn the grown-ups.

When I saw them, I stopped. I wanted to scream that something awful had happened to Roop, but they all looked so happy that it didn't seem a good idea. They'd surely only laugh!

They asked me if I wanted another drink, and I said 'No, thank you,' and had they seen Roop?

One of the larger Brats wandered in with an empty plate. On being questioned, he reported that Roop had complained of being too hot and said he was going to get some water to cool himself.

I jumped a mile, because I thought I knew what Roop had meant, but the others didn't seem worried.

Aunt Martha got up and stretched and said she'd better take that boy's temperature now.

I looked at Mrs Hood, and she wakened from smiling content to fear. She stood up, shouting something, but I didn't wait to hear what it was. I couldn't wait for anything or anybody. I ran down the path, brushing past Clemmie, who had darted out and was trying to stop me, wanting me to play some game with her . . .

. . . down through the shrubbery . . .

. . . through the vegetable garden . . .

And there I stopped because the water was no longer slowly flowing past the lawn, but was half-way up it, and it wasn't slow any longer, but rolling fast and surging up with little wavelets that weren't green but brown . . .

The stream had flooded into a river, pounding downstream, taking with it everything that got in its path, including clumps of earth and branches of trees.

The weeds were out of sight, but I knew what they were doing. They were standing upright in the water, waving their fronds around, searching for some-body's leg to grab.

And Roop was there, of course.

I couldn't see him, but this was where he would be.

I knew it, just as I'd known something to do with water was going to come up and hit me ever since that moment in the service when I'd read the words on the wall: Living Waters.

And what I'd heard in the Bible reading: 'Fear not, when you pass through the waters, I will be with you; and through the rivers, they shall not overwhelm you.'

Could I trust what I'd heard? Would God be with

97

me if I dared to go into the water?

I thought, I *will* trust. I *do* trust. Please, God. Be with me.

I waded into the water. It plucked and pulled at me. It tried to turn me round and send me back to the bank.

I wouldn't go.

I floundered forwards and managed to grab one of the fence poles with its clinging tassel of pink roses. I clung to the post and the water tried to suck me away, to pull me away from safety.

'Jan! Oh, heavens, Jan! Come back!'

It was Mrs Hood, hands to head, screaming.

I gave her one quick look and turned back to search for Roop. I knew he must be here. He'd been hot. He'd wanted water, and he'd come down to it, to the forbidden, exciting place where cool water would be. Perhaps the stream had never flooded before while the fence was down, not in his short lifetime. He wouldn't know it was dangerous.

I looked for a clue and found it. A tuft of blue had caught in the thorns of a rose, near the edge of the water.

Roop had been wearing a fluffy blue headband of just that shade of blue. He must have waded into the water, been swept against the post and clung there for a while till his little arms had given way and the current had taken him. Where? To the opposite bank? A large branch, almost a tree, had grounded not far downstream. Perhaps he'd been caught in that. Was that a flash of blue I could see among its leaves? I called his name, but there was no reply . . . or was there? I could be deceiving myself, but I thought I heard a cry.

The water dragged at my legs, almost wrenching me from the post. I spotted another, smaller, branch of a tree being swept downstream towards me. I cowered close to the post, praying it wouldn't be uprooted by the impact. The branch hit us both with a thud that set the post trembling. But it held fast, and so did I. Slowly the branch swung round at an angle, and finally, reluctantly, went on its way. But as it went, rolling over, it caught the grounded branch, and together, slowly, they began to move away downstream.

Were they taking Roop with them?

'Jan, come back!' That was Clemmie. I didn't even turn my head. There was a babble of voices behind me, but I didn't have a second to spare.

I gestured for them to be silent, and they were. I thought I had heard . . .

Had I heard anything? The water was making so much noise, gurgling, sucking, rejoicing as it smothered everything in its path.

Yes, I had heard it, a tiny, pitiful cry. And a splash as a brown hand broke through the surface and vanished again.

The tangle of trees and branches swept round the corner out of sight, but I thought I saw a commotion in the water where they had been. If Roop had been clinging to the grounded branch at this end, and then it had been wrenched out of his hands by the impact of the branch coming downstream, he might still be there, caught in the weeds.

I looked at the brown muddy depths, and my fear rose up and screamed at me, You daren't! But if you do, I'll have you for good this time!

I hadn't been sure about praying before, but now

was a good time to start. I looked up at the thin blue of the sky and said, 'OK, Jesus. They said you are everywhere, even in the darkest places, and that you really care about us. Please keep me safe in the water.'

Then I let go of the post and slipped into the water. I followed Roop, letting the current take me, going under water, feeling my way before me. I couldn't see anything in that mud, but I could feel the weeds closing over me. I wanted to scream, but I knew I mustn't. I had planned to push the weeds gently apart, to work myself through them. But the water caught me and thrust me forward with such speed that I thought I would be flung against the bank downstream.

And then, just as I thought I had failed, I felt Roop's T-shirt with the fingers of my right hand. I grasped hold of it and dragged myself alongside him, flailing with my left hand, for something, anything to hang on to . . .

. . . and thought I was going, and Roop with me . . .

. . . until my head turned red and black and I was ready to give up.

I felt something grab me around my middle and was lifted up into the air. I coughed up water and mud and floundered flat along the grassy bank.

Mr Hood laid me face down on the grass and took the boy from my arms. I coughed and heaved up water. I squinted towards Roop. He was as limp as a rag doll. He looked dead.

'All right?' Mr Hood was panting, almost as exhausted as I was.

I nodded. I was breathing like a grampus. Roop hung in Mr Hood's arms, with his eyes closed. I knew

100

what must be done, but I was so drained I couldn't do it.

Mr Hood laid Roop down on the bank and started to revive him. I clung to the thick tough grass that hung on the fringe of the bank and felt the sun warm on my wet hair and shoulders.

We were on the golf course side of the stream. We were surrounded by the branches of the willow. The sunshine shone through the leaves and turned everything to gold. Even the water was brown and gold.

They were shouting at us from the other bank. Mr Hood was straining over Roop. He shouted back, short and sharp.

Someone came pounding up from the golf course, also shouting. Everyone was shouting. I shuddered and put my head down into my hands and wept.

They got Roop breathing again between them. Someone fetched a doctor from the club house, and he helped. They checked me over and suggested going to hospital, but I said no, just a good sleep would be enough. But I had to see that Roop was OK first. They showed him to me, crying feebly in his mother's arms, wrapped in blankets, before they took him off in a neighbour's car. It was quicker than fetching an ambulance.

It was Aunt Martha who gave me a bath and got me into Clemmie's bed. I was too worn-out to help myself. Clemmie hovered, with the Brats. All of them had been crying, as had Aunt Martha. But now she smiled at me; she was nice.

I wanted to go to sleep, but something stopped me. I had to tell them. I'd been living with the knowledge for so long it had poisoned my life. I clung to Aunt Martha's hand. 'They saved Chas instead of me.'

'What?'

I shook her hand with both of mine. It was so important that they understand. 'Chas, my brother. They let me go and saved him. They didn't even try. They didn't even get wet! They laughed about it, after.'

'Jan, my dear, whatever are you talking about?'

I tried to make myself clear. 'We went on the river in a punt, all of us, Mum and Dad, Chas and me. Almost exactly four years ago. It was very quiet. It was a beautiful day. Then this motor boat came down the river, very fast. There were four men in it, with music playing, very loud. They were throwing empty cans of drink into the water. Then one of them shouted that they should tie up for a while, and they steered right across our path. I screamed. Dad and Mum both grabbed Chas and then the motor boat hit us and I fell into the water. And the weeds got me.'

'But darling . . .' Aunt Martha didn't know what to say.

Clemmie hit her cheeks. 'Oh, oh!'

'They didn't even get wet. They used to laugh about it, afterwards. How they didn't even get wet.'

'But they dived in after you, surely?'

'No. One of the men from the motor boat did that. He did the first aid on me and stayed with us, helping us get back to the car, afterwards. He wouldn't go till he'd seen I was all right. He said he was so sorry.'

There was quite a silence while Aunt Martha and Clemmie looked at me with sorrowful faces. They knew what I meant, that my parents had chosen to save Chas, and to let *me* drown.

'I'm sure it wasn't the way you remember it, child,' said Aunt Martha. 'Nobody lets their child go into the water like that.'

I smiled to show I didn't care all that much—although of course, I really did—'They laughed about it, after.'

'You can laugh to cover the fact that you were dead scared, honey. I dare say in days to come we'll laugh and scold Roop for the terrible fright he gave us. Right at this minute, if I had him in front of me, I don't know whether I'd spank him or hug him. It don't mean nothing, that sort of laughter.'

'It meant something to Jan,' said Clemmie.

I was grateful for her understanding. She took one of my hands and began to stroke it. She stroked it till I fell asleep.

When I woke, she was sitting beside me, reading a book. One of the Brats was on the floor beside her, watching a portable TV with the sound turned low. It was nice to wake up to.

The air was still and the sky was turning gold in the sunset. I thought, under the willows the air had been gold with joy.

'Roop?' I said.

Clemmie jumped half out of her skin and then grinned. 'Fine. They're keeping him overnight to check that his temperature's OK. Mum's staying with him. Dad's gone over to your place to tell your parents what's happened, and Aunt Martha's cooking supper. How do you feel?'

'Fine.' I wasn't fine. I hurt all over, but no more than when I'd fallen down the stairs.

It was enough to be warm and safe and yes, loved.

Then I heard my mother's voice as she came up the stairs, and I knew I didn't want to see her, ever again.

11

A Better Understanding

I was too old to retreat under the bedclothes. I sat up, wincing at all the bruises I'd collected.

She swept into the room projecting her anger in front of her. It was all I could do not to press back into the pillows.

'Darling, are you all right?' Her voice was honey, but I could feel the tight-lipped anger behind it.

I nodded.

She bent over me, felt my forehead, and tutted over the mess my hair was in. 'When we got home and saw Mr Hood's car outside, I nearly fainted! I just knew something awful had happened . . .'

'She saved our Rupert's life,' said Aunt Martha, giving me a loving, meaningful look.

'What a little heroine she is, to be sure!' said my mother. The edge in her voice must have been as clear to Aunt Martha and Clemmie as it was to me, for they looked at one another, quickly, dartingly, and then looked at me with identical amused expressions.

I didn't understand at first why they were amused. And then I realized they thought my mother was angry because I'd frightened her. I wasn't sure that was why she was angry, but I said to her, 'I'm fine. It was nothing.'

I got out of bed rather awkwardly and slid into my clothes, which had been washed and dried for me while I'd slept.

My mother caught me up in a fierce hug. That hurt so much that I nearly cried out. Maybe she did love me, after all. She asked Aunt Martha, 'And the little boy is all right?'

'Just fine.'

Aunt Martha kissed me. Clemmie kissed me, and so did the oldest of the Brats—temporarily ducking away from the TV to do so—and I went downstairs within the circle of my mother's arm, feeling unreal.

Mr Hood was in the hall. He put one hand on my head and the other on my shoulder. He had the kindest, most serious face you ever did see.

He said, 'Thank you, child.'

I asked him, 'Are *you* all right, too?'

'Got a bruise on my leg you wouldn't believe!'

'So have I.'

Everyone laughed at that except for my mother, whose grip round my shoulders tightened. Mr Hood bent and kissed me on the forehead and led us out to his car. I got in the back, my mother got in the front, and we drove home with them making polite conversation.

Dad and Chas came into the hall when we got back. 'Here you are at last!' said Dad. He patted my shoulder. Then he shook hands with Mr Hood and thanked him for bringing me safely home.

Chas' eyes were bulging so much I thought they'd pop out of their sockets. I said I wanted some milk to drink and went into the kitchen. Chas followed me.

'Did you really rescue someone from drowning? Really truly?'

'Yes, but I couldn't have got out if Mr Hood hadn't dived in after us.'

'Wow.' He was impressed. He made as if to touch me but didn't.

Something occurred to me. 'Chas, do you remember the day I nearly drowned in the river?'

He looked puzzled. 'You mean, today?'

'No. Before. When you were little.'

He shook his head, frowning. 'No. How little was I?'

He'd been four, only a little older than Roop. Too little to be able to swim. I'd forgotten that. Of course the reason Mum and Dad had grabbed Chas, was that he wasn't able to swim by himself, and I had always been a good swimmer; till the weeds got me. It had been unreasonable of me to think they'd loved Chas more because they thought of saving him before me.

I felt a marvellous sensation of release. It occurred to me that maybe I'd grudged Chas the fact that the parents had grabbed him instead of me, all these years. Silly to resent it.

I swallowed half the milk and choked.

Chas banged me on the back.

I smiled at him, and he smiled back. I thought, Chas is all right. I'm glad he didn't get thrown into the water. He'd never have made it.

He said, 'Would you like to play with my new computer game?'

I thanked him, appreciating the honour, but declining it. I'm not really into computer games.

He was still doing his frowning act. 'Do you mean that old story about you falling overboard and being fished out by a holiday-maker? I thought it was just a story.'

'No, it really happened.'

'But you're such a good swimmer!'

I nodded. I thought Mum and Dad had probably relied on that, too. Something tense eased up inside me. Had I been hating them for nothing?

What was it I'd just thought?

'Hating them'?

I didn't hate them. Of course not.

Chas steamrollered his way out into the garden where one of his friends was waiting to play with him. I thought I might as well go upstairs and wash my hair, which felt awful. The living room door was open a little way and I could hear them arguing inside. Well, not arguing, exactly.

Mum was sort of laughing, only not as if she were amused. More as if she were trying not to scream, and Dad was talking to her, gently, reassuringly.

I didn't mean to listen. I just heard.

'. . .and to think we nearly lost her, all over again!'

'Come on, now,' said my father. 'It didn't happen. You shouldn't let yourself get so upset.'

'But she could have *drowned!* It brought it all back! And the little boy is still in hospital!'

'Now you know they said he was going to be all right, that they didn't anticipate any after-effects . . .'

'I can't help it! When Mr Hood said there'd been an accident and Jan had gone in to rescue his little boy, I was sure she was dead! Why we ever let her go near water again, I don't know!'

'You know we agreed it was a good thing for her to continue with her swimming, if she wanted to. And look how well she's done with it! You really must try not to blame yourself. We both did what we thought was right at the time, and there was no harm done, now was there?'

'I should have asked if there was any water at the Hoods', before I agreed to her going there!'

'Now you're being absurd. My darling, stop blaming yourself for everything. Jan is all right, she's a little soldier . . .'

Little does he know, I thought!

I crept up the stairs and into my bedroom. I felt strange, kind of floaty, too tired to think straight.

I looked at myself in the mirror and wondered what a drowned person looked like. I ought to know. My hair looked awful. But instead of doing something about it, I fell on to my bed and went to sleep.

I didn't go to school next day. As a matter of fact, I didn't wake up properly until ten o'clock in the morning. Mum had come in when it was dark, removed my outer clothes and tumbled me into bed. I'd slept right through.

I felt all right, but I didn't get up for a long time. I had a lot to think about.

And as I lay there, I stretched out my legs and arms and it felt as if I'd grown a couple of inches overnight. I sighed and closed my eyes and wriggled myself flatter on the bed. Everything felt good, the bed, the pillow, the duvet.

I thought, Thank you, Jesus.

I opened my eyes and watched the sunlight reflect on the ceiling. The net curtains shifted in the breeze from the half-open window, and the sunlit reflection shifted like water on the ceiling. Like a reflection from water. It reminded me of the promise in the Bible reading.

When I had been in the water, Jesus *had* been

there, too. And I was safe, and so was Roop.

Thinking of Roop, I needed to know that he was all right. I showered and washed my hair thoroughly, put on clothes that didn't remind me of what had happened, and went down into the kitchen.

Mum was baking. She has a flurry of cooking now and then, when she gets guilt feelings about not being a full-time mother and housewife. Her part-time job at the charity shop often takes up more time than she means to give, and then she worries that she's not providing us with enough home cooking.

'You should have stayed in bed.'

'I'm fine, really. How's Roop?'

She was looking tense, checking me over to make sure all parts were in working order. I grinned and dipped my forefinger into the uncooked cake mixture in the bowl.

'Oh, you!' she said and slapped my hand away. 'Young Rupert's all right. He's going home this afternoon.'

We were easier with one another than we had been for ages.

Clemmie came round after school, with Lisa and her cousin.

Before I said anything to the others, I pulled Clemmie into the downstairs loo so that I could speak to her in private.

Clemmie seemed to have the same idea. 'Jan, are you all right?'

'Yes, I really am. Clemmie, please don't tell the others what I said about the boating accident, will you?'

'No, of course not. I wouldn't, anyway.'

'We'll talk about it later.'

Then I had to say all over again to the others that I was really all right and, in fact, better than usual.

Lisa's cousin had been at the party, too. He was rather nice, with a perky look to his eyebrows that fascinated both Clemmie and me. He hung around at the back of the hall till we decided to play impromptu badminton on the back lawn, and we dragged him in to make a foursome.

His name was Lee, and he was science-mad. Later, he beat Chas on one of the computer games, but we beat him at Scrabble.

Just when I thought Nicola's rejection had shattered my world, everything seemed to be changing for the better.

Tuesday morning, and Dad dropped Chas and me off at school. I had only missed one day of school, but it seemed as if I'd been away for weeks. All my problems still lay ahead, waiting to be solved. How was I going to feel when I was faced with getting into water again? How was I going to manage that speech at assembly, getting Dad's tapes back from Kerry . . . Nicola?

Clemmie caught up with me at the entrance to the swimming pool.

She asked, 'Well, are you feeling up to it?'

'Sure!' I said, though I wasn't really sure. Not at all.

Nicola was there, working with Debbie. Nicola scowled at us and didn't speak. Debbie was looking tense. Perhaps Nicola's solo wasn't going too well.

'All right?' Clemmie signalled to me.

I nodded. There was a tight place in my stomach.

but the water looked like swimming-pool water, and not like a river full of weeds. I reminded myself that God would be with me in the water, too. And stepped in.

Clemmie and I practised bits of our routine over and over. We couldn't use the music when the others were there as well, all practising different routines. This was holding us up. We agreed to work on the routine on dry land with the music, to see where we were going wrong.

At lunch-time, eating our sandwiches in the sun, Lisa suggested we bought a real magnifying glass for Clemmie to use as Inspector Clouseau. She thought she'd seen one in a second-hand shop, and we arranged to go there later. Then Lee and a couple of his friends joined us, wanting to know our secrets and what we were going to do for the Gala. We refused to tell them.

Clemmie said, 'Tell you what, Jan. If you're so worried about what you're going to say about the Gala in assembly, why don't you stand up now and do your bit, and we'll tell you if you go on too long.'

Problem number two had come up and hit me. I said, 'Look, it's all right for you, but I know I'll make a mess of it. I can't think what to say. Every time I try to write something down, I keep thinking of the things Debbie said to us, and I can't get any further.'

'Like what?' asked Lee. 'Go on, it won't kill you to tell us.'

'Well, she asked us to think how it would be if we were beaten by our fathers, or hungry in a famine, or shell-shocked in a war.'

'No, she didn't,' interrupted Clemmie. 'She said, "*Suppose* you were . . ." It makes all the difference. I

111

could almost *see* the different people she was talking about. And I was watching the others, and we were each of us struck by different situations.'

I said, 'So you see, it's hopeless. I want to talk about all of them, but I know I'd just ramble and people would get bored and stop listening.'

Lee's eyebrows perked up. 'Well, look. We're all going to help, being stewards and that, aren't we Bob? Lisa? Yes, all of us will help. So why can't we help you on this, too? Why don't we all say a bit, each of us represent one of the characters?'

'It's not a play!' protested Lisa.

Clemmie was hopping up and down. 'That's it! I can see it all. Jan, you write down what each of us is to say, and I'll master-mind it, and we'll have them all in tears and reaching for their pocket-money . . .'

'For their parents' money, please. We're not talking pennies here,' said Bob, who was Lee's best friend, and a really nice-looking boy, with red hair.

'Bags be the abused child,' said Lisa, pretending to limp up and down. 'And I'll use make-up to give myself a lovely bruise.'

I felt matters were being taken out of my hands. But if it did work, it was problem number two solved. And if it failed, at least all my friends would be in the dog-house with me.

I saw Nicola hanging around the playground by herself.

I didn't go over to her.

I wondered if I should get some eye-liner to make my eyes look bigger.

12

Shake-in-your-shoes Time

Nicola walked out of the school gates some way ahead of me. She was alone. I waved goodbye to Clemmie and the others at the corner. We were all going to meet up later for a game of rounders on the Common. I was looking forward to it. Clemmie was to bring some of her brothers and I was to bring Chas and his friends if they hadn't got anything else planned.

I could have caught up with Nicola, because she was dawdling, but I didn't. I stopped and rummaged around in my school bag, pretending there was something I'd forgotten. When I looked up, she was out of sight. I knew I was being cowardly, but I just couldn't think what to say to her.

I knew what I ought to say to Kerry, but I didn't quite have the nerve to do it. He was larking about on the opposite pavement with a couple of girls from 4L. Lee and Bob had said they'd talk to Kerry for me, but I didn't think that was right. It was my problem and it was up to me to deal with it.

The two girls ran on ahead of Kerry and crossed the road by the traffic lights. Kerry crossed over to my side of the road, dodging cars. He saw me, and his eyes passed over me. I didn't mean anything to him.

I put on a spurt and caught up with him, thinking

Now or Never.

'Kerry, could I have a word?' He really was a weed, but tall with it. He wasn't anywhere near as nice-looking as either Lee or Bob. I was trying to keep super-cool, but I knew I'd gone pink. This business of accosting boys just wasn't my style.

'Mm? What is it?' His eyes had gone over the road to where another girl from school was slinking along, pretending to be Madonna in disguise. Kerry was obviously a fan of Madonna.

'This is all a bit awkward, I asked Nicola to . . .'

'Oh, *her!*'

'Yes, well. The thing is, my dad bought some French tapes for my brother and me, and I lent them to Nicola, and she says . . .'

'You *gave* them to her. She told me so.'

'I know, but . . .' My face was scarlet. It was the most embarrassing thing I'd ever had to do. I could tell by the look on his face I wasn't going to get my tapes back, either. 'I'm really sorry, but I did only lend them to her, honest.'

'She bought them with her paper round money.'

'No, she didn't. If you look, you'll see my name on them.' He said, 'So she bought them from you. So what!' He added a couple of dirty words and swung his school bag so near me I had to step back to avoid it. Then he ran off down the road, shouting after Miss Madonna Look-alike.

I was shocked.

Then I got angry.

Then I decided that I wasn't going to let him or Nicola get away with it. I'd been a doormat for everyone for far too long, and it had got to stop!

Of course, I didn't really think I'd win. I just

thought I'd have another go at him some time, perhaps when Clemmie was around to back me up.

I went back with Clemmie to her house for tea, later in the week. Roop was playing on the floor with his brothers in front of the TV. None of them was paying any attention to the TV. Roop didn't look up when I came in.

Clemmie said, 'Roop, look who's here!'

He looked up, nodded, and went back to playing with his Lego. I felt a bit hurt. But after all, he was only a little boy. They said he was just fine now, a big clingy perhaps, but that was only to be expected, wasn't it?

We went into the kitchen where Mrs Hood and Aunt Martha were preparing tea. They hugged and kissed me. They were so nice and easy to be with.

Mrs Hood said, 'You've got to put your thinking cap on, girl. Mr Hood wants to buy you a really nice present, and you're to choose what it is to be.'

'Wow! Really?'

Clemmie said, 'You ought to tell her how much it ought to cost, or she'll go mad and ask for a Rolls Royce!'

I went up to Clemmie's room with her and looked out of the window. The stream was quiet today. The fence was back in place, and there was no trace of the party.

Clemmie put her arm around me. 'Dad wanted to move after the party, but Mum said "No". She said she felt the worst had happened and we'd come through it, thanks to you. She said there's all sorts of problems and bad things in the world and we can't live in an ivory tower. She said we've just got to learn to cope with things going wrong now and again. She says the first thing is to teach Roop to swim, which is kind of funny because we can hardly get him into the bath nowadays. We have to stand him up in the shower and make sure he uses the soap.'

'He's only small. I bet he hasn't really got over it yet.'

'No, I suppose not. He woke us all up, howling, night before last. But he was all right last night.'

I knew what he felt like. Poor little Roop.

Clemmie said, 'I keep praying for him. Do you?'

'Yes.' I did, too.

'Come to church with us again this Sunday?' I shook my head, and she looked disappointed.

I said, 'I've got a reason. It's not that I don't want to come with you again, because I do. I didn't understand a lot of what went on, and I want to find out about it. But I don't want to come this Sunday. I want to watch it on the TV at home with Mum.'

'Ah,' said Clemmie. 'Good idea.'

'Clemmie, you won't tell anyone what I said, about my accident when I was little? Mum and Dad really do love me and they do worry about me, and I just didn't understand, that's all.'

'My lips are sealed.'

We played for a while and, before I went home, little Roop came and stood by my knee, looking down at the carpet and fiddling with a piece of Lego. I guessed he was too shy to ask for a kiss, so I bent down and gave him a hug. He ran off back to his toys, not smiling, but satisfied that between us we'd done the right thing. He was a nice kid, was Roop.

I wasn't sure that Mum would watch the Sunday

service with me, but I hoped she would. I turned the TV on early, pretending to be engrossed in what was on before it. Dad had taken Chas off to get something from the garden centre. Mum was in the kitchen but came in with her coffee when the service started.

She fidgeted around with the geraniums in the window while the first hymn was sung. I didn't know it, and I thought she'd probably go out in a minute. But she didn't. She sat down and started flicking through the Sunday supplement.

Someone read a passage from the Bible. They said that whatever you did for anyone in need, you did for Jesus . . . even down to giving them food. Or water, I suppose.

She leant forward and switched the TV off. I was upset but didn't show it.

She said, 'You don't usually watch that programme.'

'I went to church with the Hoods last week. It was amazing.'

'Ah. All arm-waving and singing Alleluias?'

'What's wrong with that?'

'No need to get stroppy with me, madam.'

I looked down at my hands. I'd messed it up.

Mum said, 'Did you really want to watch it? It takes all sorts. I was wrong to jump down your throat. I used to go to a church like that when I was a girl, but then I married your father and had you kids and there was always so much to do around the house. Somehow, I don't know, Sunday has got to be a day for doing family things.'

'What about Dad? Did he ever go to church?'

'I think so, when he was a scout, when he was growing up. People can believe and not go to church,

117

you know. Is that what you're getting at?'

I wasn't sure what I was getting at. We looked at one another across the expanse of carpet. I thought, we're talking adult to adult, and not parent to child. For a moment I had a sensation of vertigo, a feeling almost of panic at what I'd got myself into. At the same time I realized that I was beginning to grow up at last. When I'd gone to bed the previous night, I'd had this fantasy of running to Mum and hugging her and telling her I loved her. In my daydream, she had hugged and kissed me back, and told me that she loved me, too.

But in the clear light of morning, I knew that that sort of thing wasn't likely to happen in our family. In the Hood family, maybe. But not in ours. It wasn't that we didn't love one another, but that we didn't show it that way.

What happened in our family was that Mum put her Sunday supplement aside and prepared to talk to me on equal terms. It was a bit shattering, really.

I said, carefully, 'I've learned a bit about God's love. And about Jesus, and that believing in him makes all the difference.'

She folded herself more firmly into her cardigan, her eyes not quite meeting mine. 'Well, I suppose most people believe that.'

'Do you believe that?' She uncrossed and recrossed her legs. 'Yes, I suppose so. Yes.'

I leaned forward. 'And Dad?'

'What is this, the Spanish Inquisition? Yes, I suppose he does.'

'But Chas...'

'What you're saying is that you want to go to church again. This is all the Hoods' influence, I suppose.'

'Is that wrong?'

'No, I suppose not.'

'Will you come with me?'

'Now that's something else. We'll see.' I opened my mouth to argue, but she said firmly, 'I'll talk to your father about it, OK?' She twitched the supplement back on to her lap and opened it up. The subject was closed.

I picked up my homework, thinking, that was a good start, I don't know how I dared, but Mum didn't jump down my throat. Maybe, if she doesn't say anything to Dad, I'll be brave enough to speak to him myself. But I won't push it. If they really don't want to go to church, maybe I'll go with Clemmie.

It was Shake-in-your-shoes time. Monday morning, assembly for the whole school. Clemmie, Lisa, Bob, Lee and I waited in a line at the side of the stage. When we'd rehearsed our piece, we'd done a lot of giggling and mucking about, but there was none of that now. I hoped the others weren't feeling as frightened as I was. Debbie beckoned us onstage and said we had an important announcement to make.

The others lined up facing the back wall. I came on last and faced the school. I was trembling with nerves, but I tried to send my voice clear to the back wall.

'We are children in trouble.'

Lisa turned round to face the school. She said, quietly but clearly, 'I'm scared. My dad doesn't seem to like me. Whenever he sees me, he hits me. Last time, I was unconscious for hours. What will happen next time? I don't know where to go for help.'

I don't know what the school had been expecting,

but it wasn't that. They froze to attention.

Bob turned round. There was a rough note in his voice which conveyed desperation. 'I'm sleeping rough. I can't go back home. I'm ashamed to beg, or to steal. I reckon I've just about had it. If only there were someone to help.'

Clemmie turned round. 'We're living in a cellar, my mother, my elder sister and I. My little brother died last night. Our house is in ruins. Soon the soldiers will come and kill us all. If only there were someone to help!'

Lee's turn. 'I can't go any further. I carried Mum till she died. Dad went on ahead with my brother, but we got separated. I don't know where they are. I haven't eaten for three days. I wish there was someone, anyone, somewhere, who knew about us and could send us food.'

Everyone looked stunned.

I stepped forward. This time it was easy to send my voice to the back of the hall.

'*We* are going to help. There are people who give their lives to helping these children. Now we know about it, we can help these children, too. The Synchro-Swimming Club is going to put on a Gala at the end of term, at the Leisure Centre. The money will go to the people who spend their lives helping others. You can help, too. We need people to sell the tickets, to act as stewards and maybe even provide food and run a buffet for the interval. Debbie has got the details.'

I thought, panic stricken, that I ought not to have called Debbie by her first name in front of the whole school. It was too late to say 'sorry', so I went on: 'Will you help us,' I gestured to the others, '... to help them?'

I don't know what I'd been expecting. Smiles, and nods of agreement. Perhaps even a polite clap.

Nothing happened.

Not a thing. No one even moved.

Then H.H. said, very gently and slowly, 'I think we'd all like to help, Jan. Will all the form teachers please take names and note down offers of help to give to Miss Wright. Now can we have some music, please, to see us on our way out. Form 3L, will you lead off, as usual?'

The Head of Music started playing something soft. He usually played loud marches to see us out of assembly, but this was different. No one was marching off, today. They walked off quietly, not even trying to talk as they sometimes did.

I couldn't see very well.

Debbie came up on to the stage and gave me a hug. She was crying. Then she went along the line, hugging us all, even Lee and Bob. Lee blew his nose loudly.

Clemmie said, in a wobbly voice, 'Jan, that was ... quite. It really was.'

'Not a dry eye in the house, my dears,' said Bob, trying to pull off his usual grin but not quite making it.

I said, 'Was it all right? They looked stunned.'

'Yes,' said Debbie. 'Believe me. Yes.'

Then the most extraordinary thing happened. H.H. came up and shook hands with us, one after the other He said to Debbie, 'Of course you've invited the Mayor and our local M.P.? No? Well, I think we'd better get our heads together over the guest list. Now, if you need any help backstage, or with running the buffet, I think we can arrange something. My secretary can send out the invitations and . . .'

He walked off with her, still talking.

Lisa tried to pretend she wasn't impressed. She held up her hand, the hand H.H. had shaken, and said, 'Is this the mitt touched by royalty?'

'Daftie.'

'Come on,' said Lee, 'or we'll be late for class.'

Debbie was getting worried. Everything that could have gone wrong that week had done so. Nobody seemed able to remember their sequences, while Anoushka and Ruth had had a painful collision doing deck work, and had been unable to practice for three days.

'Listen, kids,' said Debbie, calling us out of the water early. 'Let's just stop there, shall we? If we go on, we'll only make matters worse.'

We crawled out and trudged along to the changing rooms. An air of depression hung over us all as we showered and towelled dry. There was hardly any talking.

'I've ordered hot drinks all round, my treat,' said Debbie, reappearing with a trayful of cups containing hot chocolate, tea and coffee. 'So let's all sit down and relax for a change.'

I perked up immediately, but Clemmie still looked moody. She'd been mistiming her moves in the Pink Panther routine the last few days, and I knew she was about ready to give up.

We got outside those hot drinks as quickly as we could. Debbie was right, and they did help. Ruth even smiled for the first time in ages. Nicola was looking down into her cup. I noticed that nobody much was talking to her nowadays. I was sorry about that. Sort of.

'Now,' said Debbie. 'Do you want the good news first, or the bad?'

We all pulled faces, and Anoushka said she thought she could only manage the bad news if she had the good news to look forward to.

'Right,' said Debbie. 'The bad news is that at the moment we are nowhere near ready to perform, and the Gala is eight days away. You all know what you are supposed to be doing, but we've lost the edge which turns a competent performance into a good one.'

Clemmie and I looked at one another. We weren't turning in even a half-way decent performance at the moment.

Debbie continued, 'I know you are all tired and have had end of year exams to contend with. But the exams are over now, and I'm going to be here every day, before and after school, to help you do a bit of polishing.'

Clemmie muttered that a spot of pathology might be more to the point on our routine.

'I thought pathology was for dead things,' said Nicola, nastily.

'That's what I meant,' said Clemmie.

'Oh, come on!' I said. 'Never say die! We're not that bad!'

Nicola snapped back, 'Says who?'

Debbie intervened. 'Jan's quite right. A tweak here and a touch there, and their routine will be extremely good. That applies to you, too, Nicola. Actually, it applies to all of you, without exception. So now, would you like some good news for a change?'

13

On the Air

Yes, we certainly could do with some good news.

Debbie said, 'The good news is that we have sold nearly all the tickets, and that the home economics department of the High School is putting on a buffet in the interval for us. We have enough people wanting to be stewards and sell programmes. Ruth has got us some props, and Anoushka has got us some lighting.

'The Mayor is coming, and our local M.P., which means the local press is coming, too. We're having photos taken at the dress rehearsal and I've made arrangements to have all the good prints copied so that we can sell them on the night.'

'I'm impressed,' said Anoushka, and spoke for us all.

'And lastly, we're being interviewed on local radio on the morning of the show!'

'Phew! Who's "we"?'

'Jan is going to do it with me. We have to go to the Town Hall at a certain time in the morning, and there is a direct telephone line there to our local radio station. It'll be like talking on the telephone to someone, but it goes out live on the air!'

I was scarlet with embarrassment. 'Oh, no! Not me again!'

'Who better? You did all the work for the hot spot at assembly time, and you did it very well.'

'But all the others worked on it, too. It wouldn't be anything without them!'

'Unfortunately I can't get all of you off school for the morning. You'll have to make the best of it, Jan. Cheer up! Think what the Pink Panther would do about it.'

'He'd disappear!' I said, and everyone laughed.

'You'll be all right,' said Clemmie, as we walked home together. 'You always are.'

'So are you. I know you get these 'down' patches, but you always come up again, and I know you'll give a fantastic performance, far better than me.'

'You think so?' Clemmie perked up a bit.

'I know it. I mean, I'm sort of ordinary at acting, and I'm only just beginning to get good by copying what you and Debbie tell me to do. But you just *know* how to make people laugh.'

Clemmie sighed. 'I suppose. But don't run yourself down, Jan. It's really great working with you. It's just that I know deep down that this swimming lark is not for me. Every time we get into the water to do a big routine, I'm conscious I can't do things as neatly as the others. I still can't point my toes the way you do.'

I was silent. I knew what she meant. If I worked very hard for a couple of years, I might one day be able to do all the things that Anoushka and Ruth did, but Clemmie never would.

As we reached our house, I asked, 'Coming in for a bit?'

'No, I've got to look after the Brats while Mum takes Roop to the doctor's.'

'Nothing to do with his dip in the river?'

'No. He's got an ear infection. He gets them, sometimes. So how do you feel about water, now?'

'Nearly all right. Just now and then I panic for a moment, but well, it's different now. I know I'm safe, no matter what. It's hard to explain.'

'That's good, anyway.'

She lifted her hand and drifted off, still not firing on all cylinders. I leant on the gate and watched her out of sight, wondering what I could do to help her. I owed her so much.

Just at that moment, who should walk by but Kerry and his latest girlfriend Kate, a blonde from 4L. I remembered that she lived just off our road. Kerry must have seen me and said something to her, for she looked across at me and frowned. They stopped and began to argue. Twice she looked across at me. Kerry seemed to be urging her to walk on, but she wouldn't.

Suddenly Kate looked both ways and walked across the road to me. Kerry stayed on the other side, banging his bag against the wall of the nearest garden.

'Hi,' she said. She'd never spoken to me before.

I said, 'Hi,' back, being polite.

'I think these are yours?' She held out my French tapes.

'Yes, they are. Thanks.'

She fidgeted a bit. 'I heard, that is Kerry said . . . there are all sorts of stupid rumours going around but I honestly don't believe that Nicola stole them.'

'Oh, no. She didn't. I lent them to her.'

'Good. Some of our crowd said we should send her to Coventry, but I said we shouldn't do that to anyone. Right?'

'Right. I *did* lend them to her, and then she lent them to Kerry. Only he didn't seem to understand that they weren't hers to give away.'

'That's what I thought. He's a bit of a prat, isn't he? He said he was giving them to me, and in the same breath asked if I'd go with him to the disco at the Youth Club. Boys! Do they think we're stupid? Don't answer that!'

I grinned back at her. 'Thanks for giving them back. Dad bought them for my younger brother and me, and my life wouldn't be worth living if I didn't hand them on to him.'

'Oh, you've got a younger brother, too, have you? A pain, aren't they? Mine's eight and totally horrendous.'

'Probably a bosom pal of my brother.'

'Perhaps they deserve one another.'

She lifted her hand and moved off, ignoring Kerry. He watched her out of sight and then turned round and went back the way he'd come. So another little romance bites the dust. I liked Kate. Maybe I could ask her round some time.

The Day dawned at last. I hadn't slept well. The last eight days had crawled by, but the previous night and the dress rehearsal had passed in a fast blur.

The Gala was twelve hours away, but before that was the even bigger hurdle of the radio broadcast. I didn't know which terrified me more.

I got out of bed slowly. There was no last-minute early morning practice. Just as well. My body felt like lead.

Chas kicked the door open and came in with a mug of tea.

He'd never done that before. He put it on the bedside table and looked at me, more worried than pleased with himself.

'Is it all right?' he asked. 'Milk, no sugar?'

'Sure. Thanks. What's got into you?'

'Well, they say the condemned man eats a hearty breakfast.'

I sipped the tea. I'd never had tea in bed before. I wasn't sure I liked it. Suppose I spilt it in the bed?

He was fidgeting. Something was going on in what passed for his mind.

He burst out with it. 'Jan, do you really *like* swimming?'

I stared at him. 'Yes, of course. Would I do it, otherwise?' Actually, I knew I wouldn't do it, normally. It was fear which had driven me to it, and now that fear was leaving me, I had to ask the question myself: did I really like swimming? And the answer was, no, not much.

So, a moment later, I said, 'No, not much, Chas. I'm thinking of doing something else next year.'

He looked a lot happier. 'Such as?'

'Oh, ice skating, abseiling, rugger . . .'

He grinned. 'Be serious.'

'Tennis?' Now there was a thought. Perhaps I could take up tennis seriously. With Clemmie. Did she like playing tennis? I must ask her. But first I had a small problem to sort out.

'Chas, don't you like swimming? Is that what you're getting at?'

'I hate it. Mum and Dad are always saying, "Of course you like it, of course you're going to be good at it, look at Jan!" But I hate it, really. I'm going to drop it next year, when I can choose what to concentrate

128

on. I'm going to go for football.'

'It's not because of the accident, is it?'

'No, I don't think so. I can swim all right, just as well as the others, if not better. But it seems like a waste of time, swimming up and down, up and down, counting the lengths, boring! I'd rather do something *with* other people, you know? In a team. You won't be upset if I drop swimming, will you?'

So that was it. How simple it all was, when you got to the bottom of it. 'No, of course not. Boys don't do synchro-swimming, anyway. I'm sure Dad'll be pleased if you do football.'

He grinned at me and pounded out, leaving the door open. I drank the rest of my tea and got violent indigestion. How on earth was I going to cope with that radio broadcast?

We went into the Town Hall and Debbie signed us into a special book at Reception. Then we were given a key and traipsed around looking for Room K. We found it eventually, tucked away at the end of a corridor. There was a red light on above the door and a sign saying, 'Do not enter while the red light is on.' We waited and presently the light went off, and two men came out, looking pleased with themselves.

One of them seemed to be expecting us and ushered us into the room, which was fitted out as a studio with special sound-proofing, lots of boxes and wires and microphones and things. There were also several telephones.

The man gave Debbie a sheet of instructions, told us to lock the door after him and went out. Debbie locked the door. She was as pale as I was. Both of us were breathing fast. We looked at one another and laughed, which helped.

One of the phones rang, and we jumped a mile. Debbie picked the phone up, and someone at the other end told her what switches to press on the box in front of her. Then I had to pick up a phone, too. The interviewer—it was a woman with a friendly voice—asked me a few questions about my age and what my name was. She said I was to speak up a bit but that would be all right.

She just chatted to us about how we'd come to think of the Gala, and what synchro-swimming was all about, and what the International Children's Fund did. She was really easy to talk to. Debbie relaxed and was laughing and talking quite naturally. Then the interviewer wanted me to tell her all about the Pink Panther routine, and what we did in it, and that was easy and great fun, too. Suddenly she said, 'Well, that was really good, and I think I've got enough now. Will you just hold on a moment while I check that I've got it all?'

There was a short pause, and then she came back to us to say that everything was just fine, and she wished us all the best for the Gala.

That was all there was to it. We put the phones down, turned off various switches, unlocked the door, and stepped out into the corridor.

'Phew!' said Debbie. 'I'm glad that's over.'

'When will it go out?'

'Later on this morning. They take snippets of talks from all over and put them together into a sort of magazine programme. We can listen to it in my car, going back to school. But first, let's go and have something to eat. I was too nervous to have any breakfast.'

'Me, too.'

Somehow, the Gala seemed too far off to worry about, when we'd just done the broadcast.

Later, of course, it was different. I've never felt so nervous in my whole life as when we were dressing for the show, not even when waiting to do the spot in assembly. So many important people were coming! The Mayor, the local M.P., the press! Suppose we did something stupid and let everyone down! And so many of our schoolfriends would be there, watching or acting as stewards. And the people who'd slaved to get the buffet together.

I felt sick.

'It's a full house!' hissed Lisa, who'd been out to peep at the audience. I was ready, so I shot out to have a peep, too. The parents and Chas had good seats just behind the V.I.P.s, and the Hoods sat nearby. H.H. stood up as the Mayoral party came in. Anoushka presented a bouquet to the Mayoress and Ruth gave one to the lady from the International Children's Fund. Everyone settled themselves to watch.

'Ready?' said Debbie, watch and clipboard in hand. She looked rather pale. Looking around, I noticed that everyone looked pale, too, under their make-up.

We lined up, red team to the right, black to the left, and waited for the music to start.

The first routine was based on easy movements, but looked spectacular because of the way it had been choreographed. The black team danced on to the deck under the clock, while the reds turned left and lined up opposite the Mayor and V.I.P.s.

Anoushka led the reds and Ruth led the blacks. We

held our poses to a count of five and then Anoushka and Ruth stepped into the water, and we all followed suit, one after the other. Clemmie and I were last in.

Then we did formation work, criss-crossing one another in lines across the pool. Then the blacks dived and came up behind the reds, and vice versa. We swam in arrowhead formations, and then in lanes. The red teams sculled while the blacks did ballet legs, and so on. We swam to some fast jazzy music, finishing up in a giant circle which we held till the lights went off, and we swam for the sides.

With that sort of routine you don't think of yourself as an individual but become part of the squad.

It worked well, and we got a terrific boost of confidence as we heard the first round of applause.

I suppose most of the audience might never have seen synchro-swimming before, and would have been struck with the beauty of it, something we had rather taken for granted in all the months we'd been toiling away at it.

We ran down the corridor into the changing room and met Celia coming up. She was ablaze in dark blue shot with Lurex threads and wore a sequinned head-dress. She looked terrified. The volume of continuing applause for the introductory number seemed to reassure her, and she ran on with a big smile and posed at the head of the steps. She had worked out a fantastic solo to one of the themes from *The Snowman*.

'That was really good!'

'They did seem to like it, didn't they?'

Debbie popped her head round the door. 'Hush! No talking! They can hear you out there!'

We towelled ourselves dry and changed into our

next costumes. I helped Ruth and Di get into the costumes for their duet. They were so nervous, their teeth were chattering.

When they went out to wait for their cue, I saw that Nicola was sitting in a corner with her head in her hands.

Celia came back looking radiant, whispering that they were a lovely audience and it was just marvellous!

The others weren't watching, but I saw Nicola slip through the door that leads to the toilets. I tried to catch Clemmie's eye, but she was doing some limbering up exercises and didn't notice. So I followed Nicola.

She had pulled off her costume and was putting on her outdoor things. She couldn't be planning to leave now, could she?

14
The Gala

I checked that the door to the changing room was shut. I didn't think I was wise enough or clever enough to deal with this, but there was no one else around.

'Nicola...'

She jumped. 'Go away!'

'Nicola, what are you doing? You can't leave now, right in the middle. The routines won't work if you drop out. All the numbers would be uneven. And there's your solo.'

'I don't care. I can't go out and do a solo in front of all that lot. I just can't, and you can't make me.'

'Look, I know we've not been friends lately, but...' I was going to say, 'If I can help in any way...' Then I realized I couldn't say that. I'd always been trying to help her, and she hadn't liked it. Perhaps I'd gone the wrong way about it. I *wanted* to help her but just didn't know how to do it.

'I know I'm letting them all down, but I can't help it. It's not just stage fright, it's everything. Oh, go away. I hate you!' She pulled on her jumper and ran her hands up through her wet hair.

Well, that was a slap in the face, but no more than I'd been expecting from her. I said, 'Look, I know about your Dad. I'm sorry.'

'You're always saying you're sorry. It doesn't mean anything.'

I bit back a sharp word. 'OK, so I'm tactless.'

'You certainly are.'

'And maybe I didn't always go the right way about showing that I liked you . . .'

'No, you didn't. You were always trying to bribe me, giving me money. Money doesn't mean anything to you. You've got so much.'

'But I don't get that much! You know I have to do household chores to earn it. I don't get nearly as much as some people. Only, what I did get, I wanted to share with you.'

'Well, I get even less than you do, and I have to do a paper round to make up, and then I have to buy lots of things for myself out of it.'

'And that means we can't be friends?'

She stepped into her trainers. 'Not any more, no.'

'What's so different now?'

'You know. They all look at me now as if I were dirt. If it weren't for you, they wouldn't know about Dad, or me needing money, or anything.'

'But I didn't tell them. I didn't know for ages.'

'I don't believe you.' She bent down to lace up her trainers.

'I think you do. I think you were angry and upset at what had happened at home, and you took it out on me.'

'I was tired of going about with you. You're such a wimp!'

I swallowed some more sharp words. 'Well, maybe I am and maybe I'm not, but I was your friend and I'd have stuck by you, no matter what.'

'Even after I took that money and your tapes?'

'Yes. Friends do.'

'Well, I'm no friend of yours any more, so get that into your thick head, will you? I'm fed up to the back teeth with you doing your saintly act.'

I turned my back on her. I was so angry, I wanted to hit her. It was all so *unnecessary*. I was going to walk out and leave her when I remembered about God also being there with us. I couldn't help her, but maybe he could. I didn't say anything out loud, but I sort of muttered something about not knowing how to help Nicola, so could he do so, please? After that I just stood there, looking at the wall. If she did walk out on us, I'd have to go and tell Debbie about the latest catastrophe. But maybe Nicola wouldn't.

There was a long silence. I could hear, faintly, applause from the pool as the duet finished. Or maybe it was after the quartet had done their 'Bolero' routine. I'd lost track of time. All I knew was that soon we'd be lining up for the flower routine which brought the first half of the programme to an end, and Nicola was still in her street clothes.

'Why don't you go?' she said.

I didn't turn round. 'I'm waiting for you. I know you're not going to let us down, no matter how awful you feel about everything.'

'You don't have the slightest idea how awful I feel!'

'I've a pretty good idea.'

'Now you're going to talk about your phobia, I suppose.'

'No, that's pretty well over.' To my amazement, I found that what I said was true. My worst fears had gone.

'Oh. Well, you're bound to tell Debbie that I tried

to walk out.'

'No, I won't tell her anything. You've got time to change into your flower costume, if you hurry. I'll go out and tell her you had to go to the toilet. OK?'

'I suppose.'

I didn't look at her but walked out into the changing room. Celia was having trouble pinning the spray of flowers on Di's hair. I'd got mine on already. Clemmie was having trouble with hers, too, so I helped her. Clemmie was looking grim. So what was wrong with her? I didn't think I could stand another scene.

I patted her back and said, 'All right?'

She nodded but didn't smile. She was a lot stronger than Nicola. She'd cope, somehow.

Nicola had slipped back into the changing room and was now struggling into her flower costume. I heard her whispering to Ruth that she'd had to go to the toilet. She only just made it in time. Debbie signalled for us to go on.

This time we all ran out together and created a tableau in front of the V.I.P.'s chairs. We were wearing sweet pea colours. Some of us had costumes with a lot of green in, and the others wore costumes which were mainly either pink or lilac. Anoushka was the Queen of the Flowers, with a vivid deep-rose costume, and we all grouped around her.

We dived into the water in three lines, and regrouped into a flower formation. There was applause at the effect. Then we changed into another formation, and Anoushka, who'd been waiting to one side, swam underwater and shot up through the middle to yet more applause.

I was in green, and so were Clemmie and Nicola.

We worked mostly on the outside of the flower formations, holding one another's hands to make a tight circle, or spreading out and sculling with our feet pointed inwards. Every time we moved to another shape, the pattern of colours in the water changed, and there was more applause. Once Clemmie swam out of line, and I saw her bite her lip, but she got back in pretty quickly. Nicola's face was expressionless.

We finished up with three different circles on the water, each surrounding one of our best swimmers. It was all good stuff, and we felt we'd done pretty well for the first half.

I couldn't face eating in the interval. Neither could Clemmie. Nicola did. No one would have thought, to watch her chatting with Ruth and Di, that there had been anything wrong with her.

Clemmie just said, 'Are you feeling sick? I am.'

'Ought we to go and see the parents?'

'No. Not till after.'

That was OK by me. We sat side by side in the changing room, reading a comic. Comics are good carbohydrate reading. We even laughed at one of the Garfield cartoons.

Then it was time for the second half. The opener was an eightsome reel for all the older swimmers, and was followed by Nicola's solo.

We all said, 'Good luck!' to Nicola. She grinned and said she was going to wow them. Clemmie and I didn't watch, because we were getting ready for our comedy act. No one else was doing a comedy act. I wondered if we'd been completely stupid to try one. Perhaps the audience wouldn't understand that it was meant to be comic and wouldn't laugh.

My shocking-pink swimsuit looked fine, and the ears were firmly fixed, so that they couldn't possibly fall off.

Clemmie's Inspector Clouseau cape was made of such lightweight nylon that it floated around her, while her deerstalker hat was made of lightweight plastic. She had a magnifying glass on a lanyard around her neck, knotted so that she couldn't lose it.

We looked at ourselves in the mirror. Had we made the most terrible mistake? Clemmie was shivering with fright. Surprisingly enough, I was quite calm. I must have used up all my energy in being frightened and worried about other things that day.

Nicola came back, smiling. She said it had gone much better than she'd expected. The applause she got was pretty good for someone who was really just a beginner.

Then our music began. Clemmie made her grand entrance, loping around the pool, pretending to look for footprints and tossing her cape back now and then. The audience was terribly quiet, perhaps wondering what on earth was going on. Then I shot up from behind one of the plant troughs and did my silly dance, going ever so slightly over the top with it.

There was a ripple of amusement from the audience, quickly turning into a roar as a child's voice cried out: 'Look out! He's behind you!'

Clemmie played up beautifully, wheeling around as I ducked down. The audience laughed again. Two other children spotted me crawling along the ground and called out, 'Look behind you!' And from then on, it was all systems go!

Clemmie crashed into the water and floundered

around, while I did my jazz dance act on the side. The audience laughed so much we could hardly hear the music. Every move that we'd rehearsed turned out to perfection. I somersaulted and came up behind Clemmie. She swirled round and round trying to spot me. I did a ballet leg and sank to the submarine position, circling around her with just my foot showing, and the audience went mad! Clemmie got right into the spirit of things and began shouting back at the audience, 'Where is he? There?'

And the children shouted back. It was like a pantomime act. It was terrific!

When we finally staggered out of the water—on opposite sides, of course—there were cries for an Encore and, though we bowed and bowed, they didn't want to let us go.

I'd never felt like that before in my whole life.

It was fantastic.

We retreated to the corridor, but Debbie motioned us back to take another bow. Pure magic!

Everyone patted us on the back as we went back into the changing room and said things like, 'That was brilliant!' Even Nicola, who'd not joined in the chorus of approval, eventually turned her head long enough to send me a smile of sorts.

I was glad about that. I didn't think we'd ever be really good friends again, but at least the feud was over.

Only when I was towelling myself dry did I notice that my goggles were still sitting on the bench. I'd done the routine without them!

I picked them up and swung them to and fro. I didn't need them any more.

Clemmie collapsed on to the bench and said, 'Am I

glad that's over!'

'Mm.' I sat down beside her. 'Clemmie. Do you like tennis?'

'Sure. I often play in the holidays. I used to play with Lisa, till she got on to this athletics kick. Do you play?'

'I haven't much in the past, but I think I'd like to. If your dad really meant it about buying me a present, do you think he'd buy me a tennis racquet? I did have one but Chas borrowed it and then left it out in the rain. But if your dad were to buy me a new one, then you and I could practise in the holidays and, if we're any good, perhaps we could do tennis next year instead of Synchro.'

'You at the net, and me on the base line. That might be really good.'

She perked up then, and we got ready for the finale while Di and Ruth and a quartet did their thing. Nicola sat near us, fiddling with the gold leaves that we were to wear in our hair for the last number. She looked at me and half smiled, so I went over to fix the leaves for her. Later, while Nicola went to peep out at Anoushka's solo, Clemmie asked me if I was going to be friends with Nicola again.

'Sort of.' I sighed. 'It won't ever be the same as before. But it's silly to hate her.'

The applause following Anoushka's solo was terrific. She was some performer, a real star in the making.

'One day I'm going to be like that,' said Nicola to us. Her eyes were shining.

Clemmie and I looked at one another and hid smiles. We weren't competing.

Then suddenly it was time for the finale. It was

almost dark outside by now. The sky above the glass roof had clouded over. The lights dimmed, and the slow Tchaikovsky music started to play. Anoushka rushed past us to do her quickest change of the evening, and a general murmur of anticipation went through the audience.

The art department had fixed night lights on square plastic floats for each of us. As we lined up, Lisa and Debbie went along with tapers, setting the night lights aglow. Then we paced out on to the deck until we formed a ring round the pool. For a couple of bars we circled our partners. Setting the floats down, we sat on the edge of the pool and slid into the water. Retrieving the floats, we swam to the centre in a star formation. Everyone clapped.

Everything we did seemed to work. We'd practised the movements many, many times without the night lights, and in daylight. Debbie had told us it would be magic at night, but I don't think we'd realized just how dramatic it would look.

When we'd gone through our routine, the music changed.

We all looked up, raising our right hands to point at the centre of the roof overhead. We were nervous because things had always gone wrong at this point before. The wires had got tangled, or the weights had been uneven. Anything and everything.

I knew Lee and Bob were up on the balcony, helping Anoushka into the swing. They were in charge of the ropes, and they were both sensible people, but . . .

There was a sigh from the audience as a gold-painted swing, decorated with gold roses, swung out and down from the balcony. Anoushka stood on the swing, holding on to one of the ropes, waving at us all and smiling. She was wearing a gold costume covered by a spangled net robe that swayed and billowed as she descended, slowly, gently, through the air. The swaying of the swing stopped as Lee pulled gently on the guide rope.

We were all glad that Anoushka was such a good swimmer. If something had gone wrong and she'd fallen off from that height, then she would *need* to be a good swimmer.

Suddenly someone began to clap. We were sculling below her in the water, smiling up as she waved and waved again, blowing kisses all round.

The music stopped, she shed her robe—which had been carefully secured to the swing so that it could not fall into the water—and dived right into the centre of our formation, with hardly a splash. The night lights flickered but were not extinguished.

Anoushka came straight up again, right arm pointing to the swing. We formed a guard of honour, a double line of performers for her to swim through to reach the steps.

The applause was terrific. We put our floats on the side but remained in the water.

It was the end of the Gala, and the lights had gone up, but Debbie had one last card to play.

Anoushka held up her hands for silence. She looked beautiful in her gold costume, with gold leaves in her hair.

Debbie stepped to Anoushka's side and said, 'Thank you, on behalf of the International Children's Fund, thank you for coming and for supporting our cause so generously. But remembering the children in need, we want you to give us even more than you have already. We want you to give us all the loose change you have left in your pockets. We're not going to get out of the water until your pockets are empty. We'd like you to throw your coins into the water and trust to us to get them out!'

Almost at once someone threw a pound coin into the water near me. I dived for it and came up to put it on one of the floats. Then coins began to come thick and fast, fifty pence pieces, twenty, tens, ones, everything. I groped for a twopenny piece and Ruth got it first, but there were many others tumbling down through the water and we didn't come up with just one coin after that, but with a handful!

And everyone was laughing and enjoying it.

Finally there were no more coins to be collected.

The lady from the Fund came down to shake hands with Debbie and the rest of us. She was overwhelmed, thanking us for all we'd done for the children in need.

I saw Dad and Mum and Chas and the Hoods all standing together at the back, waiting for us to finish. Dad waved at me, grinning fit to burst. He was proud of me. They all were.

There was Lee, grinning at me and shaking both hands over his head. And there was Nicola's mum, looking as if she didn't want to intrude, and my mum going over to talk to her. Maybe Nicola and I could paper over the cracks, if we tried hard enough.

I looked around the pool. I wouldn't be back inside this place much next year, but that wouldn't be because I was afraid of water. I wasn't, not any more.

There was so much else to look forward to.